TIER ZERO

Fables for the 21st Century

Sharon Ann Harper DuBois

Dedication

For Steven, who conceived it, named it, and fixed some of it.

And for Richard and for Ellen, the loyal – and loving – opposition.

Freedom lies in the eyes and heart of the freedom-holder.

If you are happy with your level of servitude, no one can tell you you're wrong.

CONTENTS

TIER ZERO

Prologue

Washington D.C.
January 20, 2029

"I, Andrew James Anderson, do solemnly swear that I will faithfully execute the Office of President of the United States, and will to the best of my ability, preserve, protect and defend the Constitution of the United States."

~~~~~~~~

"My fellow Americans: a few minutes ago, I was sworn in as your new president.

"As you know, our nation is experiencing a crisis, a crisis unprecedented in our history. Civil unrest is rampant, and none of us seems to know how to solve our problems. There are so many factions tearing apart the very fabric of our culture that no two of us can agree on exactly what the problems are, let alone how to fix them.

"I believe the fundamental question is this: Is it reasonable to expect 357 million people, 357 million people of staggering diversity, varied

opinions, *different wants and needs and priorities, to live together peacefully under one system of government?*

"And I believe the answer is both yes and no.

"During my campaign I admitted to you that bringing us together appears to be an insurmountable problem, but that I had a solution, and implementing my solution would be my first priority once elected. I am telling you today that I have already drafted, in preparation for my first full day in office, a set of executive orders which will allow us all to live peacefully together as one nation.

"I am well aware that the naysayers—the naysayers who have stood around arguing with each other, wringing their hands while the greatest nation on earth descends toward civil war and anarchy – these naysayers will complain that these orders overreach presidential authority. In response, let me just say that there is ample precedent and clear constitutional authority for the President to issue orders such as these. Let me also say that these same detractors have failed, over the past several years, to come up with any solution – let alone a better solution -- to our country's myriad problems.

"My first executive order will be to create four levels – or tiers, if you will – of citizenship. Each citizen over the age of 18 years will choose his or her tier. In addition, we will establish four more offices of Vice Presidency. The Federal Vice President will continue as specified in the Constitution, and each Tier Vice President will be in charge of one of the tiers. Moreover, each tier will have its own unicameral legislature, elected from and by the members of that tier, chaired by that tier's Vice President, and whose legislation will affect only the members of its constituent tier....

Bylaws of Tier Four
of the
United States of America

Washington D.C.
Adopted January 2031

Preamble

We the citizens of Tier Four believe that all persons are created equal and must be treated as such. In order to secure the blessings of security and equality for all members of our tier, and to ensure the Common Good, we enact these Bylaws.

Bylaws

Section One – Government

1. The Government of Tier Four (hereinafter referred to as GovFour) will consist of a Tier Four Vice President and a Tier Four Senate. The Tier Four Vice President will serve as Speaker of the Senate.

2. The Tier Four Vice President will be elected by all citizens of Tier Four who are eighteen years old or older.

3. The members of the Tier Four Senate will consist of one senator from each state, who will be elected by the Tier Four citizens in the state they represent.

4. In order to ensure that all Tier Four citizens are treated equally, GovFour will control all material goods, businesses, industries, communication, and money within Tier Four.

Section Two -- Citizens

1. With the exception of a few personal possessions, all material

goods will be held in common by all citizens of Tier Four. The maximum allowed monetary value of the personal possessions owned by any Tier Four citizen will be established yearly by the Tier Four Senate.

2. All citizens of Tier Four will be provided with benefits that include furnished housing (including electricity, water, sewer services, and gas), food, transportation, daycare, education, health care, fire protection, and police protection. Other benefits may be determined periodically by GovFour.

3. All citizens of Tier Four will be assigned a job determined by their interests and abilities, and decided upon by GovFour.

4. Wages paid for all jobs will be determined by GovFour.

5. Wages paid to Tier Four citizens will be held by GovFour and redistributed to Tier Four citizens in the benefits mentioned above.

6. Each Tier Four family will be given two weeks paid vacation per year. The timing of the vacation will be determined by GovFour, and based on the needs of the industry in which the citizens are working.

7. Education of children is the responsibility of the entire Tier Four community. Pre-school through college education will be provided by GovFour. Attendance is mandatory, and no alternative education will be permitted.

8. No citizen of Tier Four will be permitted to own, carry, or maintain a firearm of any kind.

Topeka, Kansas
2041

I t had been a special day for Adam, and he had some questions he wanted to ask his mom and dad, but that would wait until they were all at the dinner table. Right now he was curled up on the couch watching his mom contentedly nurse his newborn baby sister. Henry, his little brother, was stretched out at the other end of the couch sucking his thumb.

Adam really liked having his mom home full time, but he knew that she would be required to go back to work as soon as the baby was weaned, and that had to be not more than six weeks after she was born. His mom was needed at her job at the bakery so that she could do her part to contribute to the Tier Four economy. Everyone had to do their part, because Foursies are all equal and Foursies are all responsible for each other and Foursies all look out for each other and Foursies all provide for each other.

Adam heard his father's unmistakable footsteps on the stairs, and smiled at his mother when she looked up.

"Hey, family!" said David Maxwell as he came through the door.

Adam and Henry jumped up and ran to hug their father. He hugged them back, then went to his wife and bent to kiss her. He looked fondly at the now-sleeping baby and stroked her cheek.

"So how are my two favorite girls?" It was a rhetorical question and didn't need an answer.

"Dad, I started real school today!" said Adam. "I'm not in pre-school anymore! But I have a question."

"I've been waiting all day to hear all about it, questions and all," replied David. "How about you two boys set the table, I'll help your mom finish up in the kitchen, and then we can have a good talk."

Adam and Henry ran to get the plates and glasses. The dining area was just an alcove off the kitchen, so even with lowered voices, conversations were impossible to ignore.

"David, it's feeling a little crowded around here. Five people in this tiny apartment are just too much. I've been thinking -- if we belonged to another tier, we could have a bigger apartment, or maybe even a little house," Tessie said timidly, the way people sometimes voiced blasphemies. "I know it doesn't happen often, but people do change tiers sometimes. There's nothing in the bylaws that says we can't."

"We're not changing tiers, Tessie! We've talked about this before. We have everything we need right here. Both our families have always been Foursies, and that's what we're going to stay!"

He took a deep breath. "Besides, what more do we need? We have a nice, two-bedroom apartment, just like every other Foursie family, and it's furnished! We get all the benefits -- free public transportation, free education for the kids, free medical care, free daycare while we're at work, food vouchers, clothing vouchers, guaranteed retirement income. Everything we need! And it's free! We have everything just handed to us. American Foursies are the freest people on earth!"

"It's not really free." said Tessie "It's taken out of our salaries before we see them."

"You never miss what you never had in your hand."

"If we belonged to another tier, we could get jobs that pay more, and the taxes would be smaller, so we'd have more cash."

"Get jobs? How do you know we could get jobs? As Foursies, we're *guaranteed* jobs, jobs that have been picked out especially to suit us. This is perfect for us."

"Have you thought what we're going to do with three children in one bedroom? Especially when Debbie starts developing into a woman?"

"We'll hang blankets across the room to make two rooms out of it, just like all the other Foursies with kids of opposite sexes."

Tessie was quiet for a few minutes while she tore lettuce into bite-size pieces.

"Something else happened today, and I just don't know what to make of it. While we were getting groceries at the FourStore out on Wanamaker, we ran into Sarah Reece -- you know, from Building 4 two blocks east – and she said "hi." But then she just looked at Adam and then at Henry, and then looked at Debbie and just kind of shook her head. She didn't smile or say "congratulations" or anything. Then she said, "Using up more than our share of the resources, are we?"

~~~~~~~

All Adam's neighborhood friends were Foursies. They all lived in virtually identical two-bedroom apartments within walking distance of each other, shopped at the same FourStores, ate similar food, wore similar clothes, heard similar conversations at the dinner table each evening. It had never occurred to Adam that there might be conflict among the tiers.

As soon as they were seated at the table for dinner, David turned to Adam. "Now, I want to hear all about your first day of real school. And you said you have a question."

"Yes," said Adam. "What's a 'whoresie?'"

"What?" Tessie asked, her fork poised halfway to her mouth.

"What's a 'whorsie?'" he asked again.

"Where in the world did you hear a word like that?" asked his father.

"Well, at recess today, some of the fourth-graders pulled a bunch of us new kids over to one side of the playground and asked us all what tier we belong to. Then they separated us into groups and started marching around and kind of singing,

> Onesies! Onesies! We are the funsies!
> Twosies! Twosies! Your moms are floozies!
> Threesies! Threesies! Your moms are easy!
> Foursies! Foursies! Your moms are whoresies!

"Right at first I thought that calling someone's mom a horsie wasn't so bad. But Hector told me it wasn't about horses and it was a bad word, but he wouldn't tell me what it meant."

"Onesies, huh?" Adam's father snorted. "I'm surprised they'd lower themselves enough to go to a public school."

"So what's a 'whorsie?'" Adam asked for the third time.

"Just never you mind, mister," said his mom.

~~~~~~~

The public school system had been expanded to operate year-round, with relaxed classes during the summer to accommodate the staggered two-week vacations allotted to the Tier Four families. The free day care centers were also located in the public school buildings so that the Threesie and Foursie pre-schoolers would be comfortable in the building when they became students, and so that students could safely go from day care to school and back to day care at the end of the school day.

Since the public school system was integrated among all the tiers, most of the students had at least acquaintances from other tiers, if not close friendships. They tended, as children have always done, to mirror the attitudes of their parents, and their parents' attitude toward other tiers consisted mainly of guarded tolerance underlaid with mistrust. "Stick with your own kind," while still alive and well, had little to do with colors and much to do with numbers.

EduFour kept close track of all the students in their tier. The students were rigorously screened at ages three and five to assess their potential. Those that showed promise were placed in accelerated classes. At 13 or 14, the Foursie students underwent a series of tests to further assess their potential, and to determine their preferences for employment. From that day on, their education was tailored to prepare them for the job that best suited their abilities and inclinations – as determined by EduFour. Some would leave school at 15 and enter job training for manual labor. Some would finish high school, some would go to university, and a very few would go on to graduate school and become doctors or lawyers. As always for Tier Four members, all their education was free.

And, as is invariably the case with free commodities, all choice had been eliminated.

And, no matter what profession they were engaged in, every Foursie family was provided with a two-bedroom furnished apartment, public transportation vouchers, clothing vouchers, protein food vouchers, fruit and vegetable food vouchers, grain-product food vouchers, beverage food vouchers, free medical care, free day care, and free education for their children. Every Foursie family was given the same cash allowance each week for personal use. Every Foursie family was given a paid two-week vacation every summer. Whether you were a maintenance worker or a physician, you received the same products, goods, services, and privileges as every other Foursie. If your assigned job had required you to stay in school longer than others, you should count yourself fortunate to be able to contribute more for the common good and to be able to ensure that everyone was treated equally.

Because Foursies are all equal and Foursies are all responsible for each other and Foursies all look out for each other and Foursies all provide for each other.

Seventh Congress of Tier Four
of the
United States of America
Washington D.C., 2043

"The Speaker recognizes the Senator from Arkansas."

"Thank you, Madam Speaker. As we all know, Tier Four is experiencing a dire problem. Privileged as we are to have access to the many benefits that come with Tier Four citizenship, many of the less-privileged citizens of other tiers have been posing – or trying to pose – as Foursies in order to take advantage of our hard-earned benefits. Many citizens of tiers where health care services are not provided free have acquired forged papers and presented themselves to Tier Four clinics for treatment. I understand there is a thriving industry, particularly within Tiers One and Two, which provides not only forged documents, but Tier Four vouchers for food, clothing, and transportation as well.

"Now, my fellow Foursies, our citizens work hard to earn the benefits provided to them by GovFour, and I will not stand for others who have not earned those benefits to take them away from our people.

"Madam Speaker, since the federal legislators seem to have turned a blind eye to our problem, I propose that all Tier Four citizens be equipped with a microchip to be inserted in their left forearm which contains all their personal information as well as proof of their right to Tier Four services and benefits.

"I further propose that all FourStores be equipped with chip readers which can read the microchips and let the store managers know when someone other than a Tier Four citizen is trying to present falsified documents."

The Speaker rapped her gavel.

"The Speaker hereby authorizes a committee to study the requirement for all Tier Four citizens to be implanted with a microchip as proposed by the Senator from Arkansas. The committee will consist of the Senators from Arkansas, Louisiana, Montana, and Rhode Island."

~~~~~~~

"The Speaker recognizes the Senator from Michigan."

"Thank you, Madam Speaker. My fellow Foursies, I rise today to address a problem that has been brought to my attention by many of my constituents.

"As you know, the formula for determining the benefits granted to all Tier Four citizens was determined by our first Tier Four Congress in 2031, and has been revised every other year since then.

"It's a complicated formula, and is closely tied to a number of factors. When a mother has a new baby, she is given a six-week paid leave from her job so that she can welcome her child, breast-feed the baby for the recommended length of time, and rest up from the birth. But what we sometimes forget is that while she is absent from her assigned job, her fellow workers have to pick up the slack created by her absence. In addition, her lack of productivity during that time puts a strain on the Tier Four economy.

"And we should not forget that an additional child entitles the family to additional food vouchers and other benefits, which flies in the face of the basic Tier Four precept that all Foursies are equal.

"Madam Speaker, I propose an amendment to the Tier Four Bylaws that reads as follows:

> Since all Tier Four citizens take care of each other and provide for each other, it is not responsible for any Tier Four family to have more children than the others and

thus make more demands on the common resources. Each Tier Four family may have up to two children. Upon the birth of the second child, the father will undergo a compulsory vasectomy. The mother will be given six weeks in which to wean the new baby. At the end of the six weeks she will undergo a compulsory tubal ligation."

The Speaker rapped her gavel.

"The Speaker hereby authorizes a committee to study the use of enforced sterilization of the parents after the birth of a second Tier Four child. The committee will consist of the Senators from Michigan, Oregon, Texas, and Florida."

Bylaws of Tier Three
of the
United States of America

Washington D.C.
Adopted January 2031

Preamble

We the citizens of Tier Three believe that all persons should be encouraged to reach their full potential. We believe it is the responsibility of the government to provide basic necessities for all Tier Three citizens so that they can achieve that potential without fear of poverty. In order to provide that secure environment for all members of our tier, we enact these Bylaws.

Bylaws

Section One – Government

1. The Government of Tier Three (hereinafter referred to as GovThree) will consist of a Tier Three Vice President and a Tier Three Senate. The Tier Three Vice President will serve as Speaker of the Senate.

2. The Tier Three Vice President will be elected by all citizens of Tier Three who are eighteen years old or older.

3. The members of the Tier Three Senate will consist of one senator from each state, who will be elected by the Tier Three citizens in the state they represent.

Section Two -- Citizens

1. All citizens of Tier Three will be provided with a Guaranteed Minimum Income, the amount of which will be determined at the

start of each session of the Tier Three Senate. In addition, each Tier Three citizen will receive free health care, free education, fire protection, and police protection. Other benefits may be determined periodically by GovThree.

2. A minimum wage for all employment within Tier Three will be determined by GovThree at the beginning of each session of the Tier Three Senate.

3. If a citizen of Tier Three wishes to have a job or to start a business, their income from that endeavor will reduce the amount of their Guaranteed Minimum Income using a formula to be determined by GovThree. Since employment is beneficial to the Tier Three economy, the formula used to reduce the Guaranteed Minimum Income will not cause the employed citizen to have an income less than if they were not employed.

4. In order to fund the Guaranteed Minimum Income, free health care, free education, and other benefits, an income tax will be imposed on all citizens of Tier Three. The amount of the income tax will be determined by GovThree.

5. No citizen of Tier Three will be permitted to own, carry, or maintain a firearm of any kind.

6. No law will be passed interfering with a woman's right to an abortion.

Topeka, Kansas
2045

"**S**o how did you do on the math test?" Adam asked Susannah. "Aced it, as usual?"

"Of course I did. I assume you flunked, as usual." They both laughed. Adam and Susan were both good students, especially in math, and the jokes about failing math tests were ongoing.

~~~~~~~

Susannah and Adam had attended the same day care and school as far back as they could remember. Even though they belonged to different tiers, they were best friends. Earlier that school year they had even joked about getting married one day, but they both knew better. Even at ten, they were well aware of the complications of marrying outside their own tier. And changing tiers after reaching the age of 18 was even worse.

While citizens were allowed to marry outside their tier, the various governments had deliberately made the process impossibly complicated. For one thing, every family had to be assigned to a tier. If both parents were of the same tier, the family was, by law, assigned to that tier. If it was a mixed-tier marriage, however, part of obtaining a marriage license involved declaring a tier for the new family and agreeing that both marriage partners would live by the rules of that tier. That left, for example, a Threesie living under Foursie rules. And, literally, every interaction of a mixed-tier marriage with governmental office in any tier required at least four forms filled out in triplicate.

The complexity achieved its unacknowledged purpose. There were almost no mixed-tier families.

For the first two years after President Anderson's inauguration, there had been considerable movement among the tiers, but that didn't last long. All citizens upon reaching the age of 18 were allowed to choose their own Tier, but within a few years most people were more comfortable in the economic environment in which they had been raised, and they stayed put. And while moving from one tier to another was allowed for adults, few people did so. As with religion, tier choices were being passed from one generation to the next. It was not unusual to hear someone say "Our family has been Tier Three since tiers got started," in much the same way that people say, "Our family has always been Episcopalian." Indeed, even marriage outside one's tier was not only a bureaucratic nightmare, the social condemnation was even more effective. It was socially frowned upon, just as marriage outside one's race or religion had at one time caused raised eyebrows and whispered comments. It wasn't illegal; it just "wasn't done." The Tier System had been in effect only a decade when sociologists began to comment on how rapidly it had exacerbated the nation's already-pervasive tribalism.

~~~~~~~

Susannah and Adam were sitting at the dining table in Susannah's family's small house, just a few blocks from their school and within easy walking distance of Adam's apartment. They were supposed to be studying, but, as usual, the study session had turned into a gab fest.

"What do you think you want to do when you graduate?" Susannah asked Adam.

"I'm kind of hoping to go on to graduate school, and maybe get assigned as a bookkeeper at one of the FourStores. Since I like math and all."

"I think I'd like to start a little business. You know how much I love to knit and sew. And Topeka doesn't really have a good yarn shop any more. I'm thinking about a yarn and fabric store. I want to call it *Yarn and Yardage*. There are several empty spaces in some of the shopping centers. I'll have to get a GovThree permit, of course."

"But you get a Guaranteed Minimum Income. I don't see why you'd want to work if you don't have to."

"Oh, Threesies have to work alright. The Tier Three Bylaws don't say so, but the Threesie economy would fall apart if everyone wasn't working. So the pressure to work is huge. You can go out and get a job, or you can start a business. It's really a pretty good deal, 'cause for every two dollars you earn at your job or your business, one dollar is subtracted from your GMI." She pronounced it 'gimmie,' with a hard 'g.' "So you're a dollar ahead for every dollar you earn. Some people say you're only 25 cents ahead because what you earn is taxed at 75 percent, but you're still better off. And that 75 percent is what pays for our free education and health care and all that stuff."

"It's not free if you're paying for it with taxes," said Adam.

Susannah ignored him. "But if we start a business it has to make a profit within two years, or GovFour shuts it down. See, the gimmies are just supposed to be a safety net. Mom and Dad told me they're intended to support families that can't work or have jobs that don't pay enough for them to live on. So if someone starts a business that doesn't make a profit, they might start pouring their gimmie into the business trying to save it, and that's not what the gimmies are for.

"To get my GovThree permit to start my business, I'll have to show I have some experience in the field and know something about running a business, and understand basic accounting."

Adam had stopped listening. He was stuck on the word 'profit.'

It wasn't that Adam was uncomfortable with the idea of making a profit. It was just that, growing up a Foursie, the concept of 'profit' had never come up in any conversation he had ever been part of. Foursies didn't own businesses and almost never worked in small businesses. The large FourStores where many of them were assigned as clerks, warehouse workers, or janitorial crew members may or may not have turned a profit, but that was never discussed with the Foursie workers. A Foursie who was assigned as a department manager had responsibilities that included supervising workers, tracking inventory, tracking sales volume, and ordering more merchandise from FourStore headquarters. Those responsibilities did not include being concerned with making a profit. The same was true for Foursies who were doctors, worked construction, drove trucks, worked in factories, painted houses, fixed cars, or were assigned as conductors on trains – no Foursie was ever assigned to a job that required the idea of 'profit.'

In the public schools, economic concepts were carefully avoided until high school, when students from different tiers often, if not usually, were enrolled in different classes, reflecting the different jobs and careers for which they were headed.

Susannah, on the other hand, had a full-blown aversion to the idea of "profit". Most Threesies, while understanding that a profit was the only thing that could keep a business running, still felt that it was somehow, well, unseemly. And making a large profit was positively vulgar. Ideally, a Threesie small-business owner would be able to give up the Guaranteed Minimum Income, take home a little more than the GMI, and live just a little better than most other Threesies. But not a lot better.

Adam was also bewildered by the idea of a privately-owned store. Other than a few unpleasant episodes watching his mother pay for purchases with Tier Four vouchers at one of the small specialty stores downtown on Kansas Avenue, Adam's only experience with retail had been the cavernous and impersonal barely-more-than-a-warehouse establishments favored by most Foursies. And even when he had been forced to witness his mother's intimidation trying to trade her vouchers for a few pieces of merchandise at a small store, it had never once occurred to him that the store might be owned and operated by other than one of the governments.

"So, if you own a store, will Foursies be able to shop there?" asked Adam.

"Of course, "Susannah replied. "Anyone from any tier can shop at any store. That's the law. Of course, it's best if they use cash. See, you know how you Foursies get vouchers for food and stuff? And then you get some cash for other things that aren't covered by vouchers?"

Adam nodded.

"Well, if a Foursie wants to buy food with vouchers outside a Fourstore, it's kind of a hassle for the store. The law says they have to take the vouchers as payment, but then they have to send them in to GovFour and exchange them for cash, and sometimes it takes, like, forever. And mostly the store loses money because of all the paperwork. My mom knows the people that own the specialty donut shop down on 10th Street, and she says they told her when a Foursie comes in to buy something with vouchers, they deliberately act real snotty and try to make them use cash instead. I know it's kind of mean, but you can't blame them because they lose money."

Adam nodded again. That explained a lot.

Eighth Congress of Tier Three
of the
United States of America
Washington D.C., 2045

"The Speaker recognizes the Senator from New York."

"Thank you, Mr. Speaker. Fellow Senators, I rise today to begin discussion about a serious problem that has been brought to my attention by a number of my Tier Three constituents. This problem extends to our brothers and sisters who are citizens of Tier Four as well. As all of you know, the bylaws of both Tier Four and Tier Three prohibit the ownership or carrying of a firearm of any kind. Our less enlightened neighbors in Tiers One and Two have made no such provisions for the safety of their citizens.

"As a result, it is not uncommon for citizens of Tiers One and Two to walk around, fully armed, in areas which are predominately Three and Four, and even to enter businesses usually patronized by our unarmed citizens.

"I propose a law prohibiting the carrying of firearms in areas which are predominately occupied by citizens of Tiers Three and Four."

"The Speaker recognizes the Senator from Maryland."

"Thank you, Mr. Speaker. While I am aware of the problem voiced by my esteemed colleague from New York, I would like to remind this body that, when President Anderson established the Tier System, he was clear that it was to be a system whereby all the citizens of this great country, no matter what their political beliefs, could live together, side by side, in peace. There are no areas which belong to any one Tier, and I fail to see how lines could be drawn which would clearly mark where firearms may and may not be carried."

"The Speaker recognizes the Senator from Connecticut."

"Thank you, Mr. Speaker. I agree with my esteemed colleague from New York. I, too, have heard from many of my constituents who are alarmed at the presence of armed men – and women – in their neighborhoods. But I beg to remind my colleague that federal law prohibits the legislature from one Tier passing a law which impacts the citizens of another Tier."

The Speaker rapped his gavel.

"The Speaker hereby authorizes a committee comprised of the Senators from New York, Maryland, Connecticut, and Wyoming to study this matter and report back to the entire body at the beginning of the GovThree Ninth Congress."

Topeka, Kansas
2053

"Hold on a minute, Adam, while I finish up my income tax."

Susannah clicked "SEND," and leaned back in her chair. Adam watched her while she got to her feet and started to gather up her records. He was still confounded by the very idea of an income tax. Who ever heard of taxing income?

Everybody but Foursies, Susannah had assured him the first time they had talked about it. "Everybody else has to do this every year. Well, Twosies and Threesies do anyway. The Onesies don't pay income tax, but they don't get any services, either. Your Foursie family actually pays a 95 per cent tax on their income, but GovFour just holds it out, gives them a bunch of services and vouchers and five percent of their salaries in cash, and calls it good. They don't have to file any forms like I'm doing. And you think this is bad?" Susannah continued. "You ought to see what the Twosies have to do."

"Anyway, we just have to fill out a form showing how much we earned at work, how much was withheld, and what we got from our gimmie. Just to make sure the numbers come out right, you know?"

Susannah and Adam had both recently turned 18, and Susannah had found a job as a bookkeeper for a group of small businesses at a strip mall on Fairlawn Road. She had opted not to go on to college because she wanted to spend her time and energy preparing to open her business. Her job didn't pay much, but she was learning a lot about small-business management, and she knew she would put that knowledge to good use when she started *Yarn and*

Yardage.

With her small salary and her monthly gimmie, she was able to afford a tiny two-room apartment. It consisted of one room with a sofa that opened into a bed, a kitchenette off to one side with a table barely big enough for two people, and a bathroom.

Adam spent a lot of time at Susannah's place, and he was always welcome. GovFour had determined that Adam would go on to college, so he would be spending at least two more years – maybe four more -- living at home. His younger brother Henry was 14, and Debbie was 12. The tiny two-bedroom Foursie apartment was crowded, noisy, and the blankets hung in the second bedroom in an effort to give Debbie some privacy were a joke. By contrast, Susannah's apartment was quiet and orderly. Adam felt like he could breathe when he was there.

Susannah glanced over at Adam. "By the way, how's your microchip implant?"

Adam held out his left arm so that Susannah could see the small red incision, which was healing nicely. "I guess I'm official now. There's no hassle using vouchers, and when I go to vote I won't have to show any ID to prove who I am. This thing *is* my ID."

Topeka, Kansas
The Topeka Online News Service
June 16, 2053

Breaking News:

In a surprise move today, GovThree implemented a requirement that all citizens of Tier Three have an identification microchip similar to the ones already in use by Tier Four implanted in their left forearm.

William Spencer, Tier Three Speaker, explained. "As you may know, for a long time we have been experiencing a problem with citizens of other tiers posing as Threesies in order to take advantage of our unique and generous Guaranteed Minimum Income plan. This is theft, pure and simple. People who have not worked to earn a GMI, and have not contributed to the Tier Three economy, are stealing from our hard-working Tier Three families, and we have now implemented a plan to put a stop to it. From now on, all Threesies will need to go to their local GovThree office to pick up their monthly GMI, and they will have proof, right there in their arms, that they are entitled to that money. Furthermore, all GovThree governmental offices will be equipped with microchip readers.

"This will not be cheap, of course, but we estimate that stopping the theft of GMI funds will more than make up for the projected expense. And, of course, no one can put a price on the peace of mind it will bring our Tier Three families to know their livelihood is not being stolen by those who have not worked for it."

"Considering the success our Tier Four brothers and sisters have had with their microchips, I feel certain this project will be a success."

In Other News:

Last Sunday, for the second week in a row, there has been vandalism in major cities, primarily in the south, of businesses that are open on Sundays. In Oklahoma City, a Target and several McDonalds fast food restaurants were set upon by large mobs which entered the establishments, caused various amounts of vandalism, and left just as quickly as they had come. In Selma, Alabama, the same thing happened to a Bed Bath and Beyond as well as a small privately-owned restaurant.

The mobs were reported to be chanting, "Remember the Sabbath Day, to keep it holy."

No organization has taken responsibility for the vandalism, but sources have suggested a Tier Two splinter group which wants to change the Tier Two Bylaws to reflect fundamentalist Christian principles might be to blame.

Bylaws of Tier Two
of the
United States of America

Washington D.C.
Adopted January 2031

Preamble

We the citizens of Tier Two believe that all persons should be free to live their lives as they see fit, within the bounds of decency. We also believe it is the responsibility of government to determine and enforce moral standards for the community. In order to ensure that freedom and maintain moral standards for all members of our tier, we enact these Bylaws.

Bylaws

Section One – Government

1. The Government of Tier Two (hereinafter referred to as GovTwo) will consist of a Tier Two Vice President and a Tier Two Senate. The Tier Two Vice President will serve as Speaker of the Senate.

2. The Tier Two Vice President will be elected by all citizens of Tier Two who are eighteen years old or older.

3. The members of the Tier Two Senate will consist of one senator from each state, who will be elected by the Tier Two citizens in the state they represent.

Section Two – Citizens

1. No restriction will be placed on the right of a citizen of Tier Two to buy, maintain, carry, or use a firearm.

2. No abortions may be performed on or by any citizen of Tier Two.

Topeka, Kansas
2053

"**S**o, Adam. What's the purpose of government? What d'ya think? What's it for?"

"Uh, to provide for everyone, to make sure everyone has enough, I guess," replied Adam. No one had ever asked him that question before. Truth be told, he hadn't really thought about it.

"Boy, howdy. If I didn't already know you were raised a Foursie, that would have given it away right there."

Dick Carpenter was a big, blustery Twosie with strong opinions, and plenty of them. Especially about politics. He was a realtor who was determined to be elected to the GovTwo legislature. Originally from Dallas, he had moved to Topeka so that he could be a big fish in a much smaller pond. Adam always thought he looked and sounded like he ought to be ridin' a horse alongside a herd of cattle with a bandana tied over his nose and mouth, something out of an old movie.

Dick was a true politician. He entertained a lot, usually favoring those who might be advantageous to his political career. He had met Susannah when, in his capacity as a realtor, he had helped her find her tiny apartment. Adam had come along on one of the viewing trips, and Dick found he really liked the two young people. They could neither help nor hurt his political ambitions, so he sometimes invited them to his home for an informal meal and some honest talk.

A decade older than Adam, Dick sometimes reminded Adam of his own dad, but with his big frame turning soft instead of remaining muscular. Adam's dad had a job in the stockroom of one of the big warehouses in the industrial area south of the Kansas River, and it kept him in good shape.

Adam didn't want to like Dick, but he couldn't seem to help it.

"A lot of people think the purpose of government is to do the things that people can't do for themselves individually or even in small groups. Things like national defense," Dick continued, "and that's a big part of it. But the biggest function of government is to decide who gets what. And who gets how much of whatever."

Adam assumed the "in my opinion" was implied.

"Think about it," Dick went on. "Way back when people were living in small groups and everyone built their own mud hut and went around gathering up his own food and maybe killing a rabbit once in a while, there wasn't much need for government. The tribal rules kept you from killing your neighbor unless you had a really good reason to, but you didn't need many more rules than that.

"But once the weapons got good enough to kill something bigger – an antelope or something else with enough meat to feed more than the hunter's immediate family – people had to start worrying about who got what and how much. Did the hunters get the best meat? What about the people who didn't help with the kill – the children and the old people and the pregnant women?

"It made sense to share the kill because it kept the tribe strong and healthy, but who got to decide who gets the loin and the liver, and who is stuck with the neck bones? Does the bravest hunter make that decision? Do the tribal elders decide for the group?

"That's the question every government has been wrestling with ever since. And Lord knows there have been darn near as many answers as there have been countries with governments.

"When President Anderson, back in 2029, set up the Tier System, he was setting up four different ways to handle that problem. Frankly, I don't think he knew he was doing that. He was just so terrified of the looming civil war and his inability to find a way for all the factions in this country to live together peacefully, that he grabbed the first idea his advisors handed him. And it did avert the war.

"Tier One is pretty much a free-for-all, an anarchy. GovOne is virtually non-existent, by the way. Tier Two says you can have whatever you can buy, and you can buy whatever you can get enough money to buy. Tier Three is based on the idea that the government should take care of everyone's basic needs, but you can have a little more if you are willing to work for it. And Tier Four says that everyone is equal to everyone else in every way, and everything must be shared equally. Four different answers to the question of who decides, and four different answers to the question of who gets the loin and the liver, and who is stuck with the neck bones."

"How about another beer?"

Thirteenth Congress of Tier Two
of the
United States of America
Washington D.C., 2055

"The Speaker recognizes the Senator from Mississippi."

"Thank you, Mr. Speaker. I come to this legislative body today to lay before you a matter that has been of grave concern for over a decade. The Bylaws of our great Tier Two are woefully inadequate to express the beliefs of Tier Two citizens, let alone to clearly state our purpose and take care of our needs. As all members of this body know, at every Tier Two Congress since 2045, several of my colleagues and I have introduced proposed amendments to our Bylaws. Every single one of them was voted down. We are left with only one remedy.

"Today I am proposing, nay, I am demanding, that Tier Two be split into two tiers. The current Tier Two will be known as Tier TwoA, and those of us who are leaving to form our own tier will be known as Tier TwoB.

"I have before me the proposed Bylaws for the new Tier TwoB, and I would like to share some of them with you. The Preamble will read as follows:

> We the citizens of Tier TwoB, trusting in the protection of Almighty God and asking for His blessing on this endeavor, believe that all persons should be free to live their lives as they see fit, within the bounds of decency. We also believe it is the responsibility of government to determine and enforce moral standards for the community. Those moral standards are to be based on the Christian Bible. In order to ensure that freedom and to maintain moral standards for all members of our tier, we enact these Bylaws.

"Furthermore, Mr. Speaker, Section Two, while retaining the right to gun ownership and the prohibition on abortions, will contain the following items:

Christianity is declared the official religion of Tier TwoB.

No Tier TwoB business may be open, nor may any commerce be conducted on Sundays.

Prostitution will be considered a crime.

Homosexuality will be considered a crime.

The breaking of any of the Ten Commandments will be considered a crime.

"There's more here, Mr. Speaker, but I will yield the floor if anyone wants to discuss the matter further."

"The Speaker recognizes the Senator from Kansas."

Newly elected, Dick rose to his feet to speak for the first time as a Senator. "Thank you, Mr. Speaker. I admit that I have some serious reservations about my esteemed colleague's proposal, not the least of which is the implied license to increase the number of tiers beyond measure. If every small group that disagreed with the Bylaws of their tier broke off, we could conceivably end up with half a million tiers consisting of a handful of citizens each.

"There is also the question of whether adding a tier would require an executive order by the President, since that's how the Tier System was created in the first place."

The Speaker rapped his gavel.

"The Speaker hereby creates a committee to study the proposal to create a Tier 2B. The committee will consist of the Senators from Mississippi, Kansas, Oklahoma, and Utah."

Fourteenthth Congress of Tier Three
of the
United States of America
Washington D.C., 2057

"The Speaker recognizes the Senator from Connecticut."

"Thank you, Mr. Speaker. I come before this body today with a pressing problem. As you know, our friends in Tier Four have already dealt with this same problem, and quite effectively, I might add.

"The problem, my esteemed colleagues, is that the demand for medical care in Tier Three is beginning to outstrip our ability to provide all the services our citizens want and need. I suppose that's to be expected when health care is considered to be a human right and is paid for out of the general treasury. Tier Four has had free universal health care from the beginning, but Tier Four citizens have never been provided with elective surgeries such as breast reduction or augmentation, bariatric bypass, or any of the cosmetic surgeries. I reluctantly suggest that this body pass similar legislation. It just doesn't seem right to ask one's fellow workers to pay for surgeries that are not really necessary."

"The Speaker recognizes the Senator from Nebraska."

"Thank you, Mr. Speaker. I must say that I agree with my esteemed colleague from Connecticut. The cost of medical services in Tier Three has definitely gotten out of hand. I would suggest, however, since Tier Three citizens often have jobs that pay them a salary, that our citizens be allowed to pay for elective surgeries out of their own pocket if they feel the surgery is that important."

"The Speaker recognizes the Senator from Oregon."

"Thank you, Mr. Speaker. I heartily agree with both my colleagues who have spoken on this matter today. I am going to suggest an addition to the proposed legislation, one that I know is also under consideration in Tier Four's Congress as we speak. My suggestion is that free medical care be denied to any Tier Three citizen who refuses to comply with their doctor's suggestions. If a citizen refuses to lose weight when told to, smokes tobacco, drinks alcohol to excess, refuses recommended vaccines, or otherwise fails to take reasonable care of their own health, it is unconscionable to ask their fellow citizens to pay for their health care."

The Speaker rapped his gavel.

"The Speaker hereby appoints a committee to look into the suggestions made here today. The committee will consist of the Senators from Connecticut, Nebraska, and Oregon."

Topeka, Kansas
2077

"But breast cancer is curable! A mastectomy, some radiation, chemotherapy – it's curable!"

Doctor Barry leaned his forearms on his desk and spoke calmly. He was used to dealing with anxious patients and their anxious families.

"Look, Adam, I know this is upsetting news. But let me explain it as best I can. Again. Your mother is 67 years old. We can keep her comfortable, but we can't cure her."

"Can't, or won't? I know of a lot of women who have been cured of breast cancer. My friend Hector's wife had it five years ago, and her doctor says she's cured, cancer free."

"How old is she?"

"Uh…I don't know for sure, but my age. Fourties, I guess."

"So she's still working?"

"Sure."

Doctor Barry laid his glasses on his desk, closed his eyes, and pinched the top of his nose. "Adam, please sit down. I've been your doctor and your family's doctor for several years now. Let me tell you some things that everyone seems to know instinctively, but aren't talked about in public very much.

"There's not enough medical care to go around. In fact, there's not enough of much of anything to go around. And that's true for all the tiers. It's true for the whole world in fact. Oh, there's enough food to keep everyone alive and reasonably healthy, enough places to live, enough winter coats for everyone to have one. But there can't be enough winter coats for everyone to have ten. There's not enough of anything for everyone to have all they want.

"If you took the value of everything produced by every working Foursie in the nation and divided it by the total number of Foursies – and that includes the children, students who aren't working yet, people who *can't* work for one reason or another, and the old people who have retired, what would you get? You'd get the value of everything each Foursie is entitled to. Then subtract the value of their free housing, free education, free medical care, free daycare – all the things Foursies get without question, without having to present a voucher -- and what's left?

"What do you think the Tier Four vouchers are? They represent the value of what's left, Adam. As you well know, it's not much. It's enough for food, clothing, public transportation, a few small luxuries. But it's not enough for Foursies to have a car, or a four-bedroom house. All Foursies are equal, and what Foursies are given is the average of what they produce as a group.

"Medical care is expensive. And there isn't enough for everyone to have all they want any more than everyone can have ten coats or a car. Foursies can't have facelifts or breast implants or bariatric bypass surgeries. And, by law, I cannot cure anyone who is no longer working. I can keep her comfortable, but I can't save her life. I'm sorry."

"But her first granddaughter is due next week," said Adam weakly.

"That's nice," said Doctor Barry. "I hope they name the baby after her."

Dr. Barry got up and walked to the door. "I'm sure Tessie would appreciate a visit, Adam." He held the door open.

Bylaws of Tier One
of the
United States of America

Washington D.C.
Adopted January 2031

Preamble

We the citizens of Tier One believe that all persons should be able to live their lives as they see fit. In order to secure the blessings of liberty for all members of our tier, we enact these Bylaws.

Bylaws

Section One – Government

1. The Government of Tier One (hereinafter referred to as GovOne) will consist of a Tier One Vice President and a Tier One Senate. The Tier One Vice President will serve as Speaker of the Senate.

2. The Tier One Vice President will be elected by all citizens of Tier One who are eighteen years old or older.

3. The members of the Tier One Senate will consist of one senator from each state, who will be elected by the Tier One citizens in the state they represent.

Section Two -- Citizens

1. No law shall be passed restricting the right of Tier One citizens to keep, carry, and maintain firearms.

2. All laws passed by the Tier One Senate will automatically expire six years from the day they are enacted unless they are renewed by the Senate or the law contains a provision for earlier expiration.

3. Since income taxes invariably progress from a means of funding government to a means of manipulating behavior, no income tax will be imposed on the citizens of Tier One.

4. Structures and institutions used by the general public, such as roads, libraries, and sewage systems, will be built and maintained using user fees.

5. Conditions of employment, including wages paid, will be determined by a voluntary agreement between the employer and the employee. No law will be passed that interferes with that agreement.

6. Education of children is the sole responsibility of the child's family. No laws will be passed which interfere with that responsibility.

7. No law will be passed interfering with a woman's right to an abortion.

Topeka, Kansas
The Topeka Online News Service
August 10, 2077

Breaking News:

In a vote that astonished the entire nation, GovOne today passed legislation that requires all citizens of Tier One to have microchips implanted in their left forearms. The microchips, exactly like those of the other three tiers, would contain not only identification data, but immunization information as well.

Forty-two of the 50 GovOne senators voted for the measure. Sandra Parker, leader of the Coalition for Chipping Onesies, had this to say: "We know that the microchips have been working very well for our fellow citizens in the other three tiers. Not only do they ensure that only the citizens of the correct tier vote in each election, but they keep citizens of other tiers from receiving benefits to which they are not entitled. The immunization information will also make it easier for the medical community to ensure that all citizens have received the injections that keep them and the rest of the community safe."

Unnamed sources have hinted that the GovOne senators were under enormous pressure from the federal government to pass this legislation, which flies in the face of many of the freedoms that citizens of Tier One hold dear.

News sources on Detroit, San Francisco, El Paso, and Sioux Falls report that many Tier One citizens have already taken to the streets in protest.

Topeka, Kansas
The Topeka Online News Service
September 15, 2077

Breaking News:

Tier One citizens in 42 states have demanded a recall vote for their senatorial representatives who voted in favor of requiring Tier One citizens to have microchips implanted in their forearms. Surprisingly, there doesn't seem to be a move to replace the senators who are in danger of being removed from office. If this recall movement is successful, GovOne will consist of eight senators.

Leaders of the recall movement were unavailable for comment, but one protester in Tulsa, when asked how having only eight senators would affect GovOne, remarked, "Sounds to me like the right size for a government."

Topeka, Kansas
2077

The three doctors who comprised the medical staff of the Topeka Tier Four Clinic sat around the table in the clinic's conference room. It was late Saturday afternoon, the clinic had been closed for an hour, and the rest of the staff had left for the weekend. There were three glasses and a bowl of ice cubes on the table. They had all chipped in some of their Tier Four cash allowances to buy a bottle of bourbon. It had been a tough week for all of them.

"Do you ever think about changing tiers?" asked May Wong.

Ronald Barry leaned over, poured himself more bourbon, and added a couple of ice cubes. "Often. But they've really got us over a barrel, don't they?"

"Y'know, when I first went into medicine, I thought I was doing something noble. All of us being equal and all. I'd work my butt off in medical school, then spend my life taking care of my fellow Foursies, saving lives and making everyone healthier." Sanjay Patel was on his third drink, and his words were slightly slurred. "But now I see all those Onesie and Twosie doctors playing golf over at the Topeka Country Club, living in big houses in Clarion Woods, and my wife and I are stuck in the same shitty little two-bedroom apartment as every other Foursie, and I can barely afford to chip in for a cheap bottle of bourbon. I spent a lot of years in school, and I don't get to live any better than any other Foursie who barely finished high school. It sounded all noble and virtuous and everything back then, but it doesn't feel noble right now."

"Like Ron said, though," May reminded him, "our education was free to us, paid for with the labor of other Foursies, and we signed a contract that we would never use our medical education outside Tier Four. We can leave the tier, but if we practice medicine in another tier, we can go to jail."

"And we're not trained to do anything else," Ron said. "I mean, seriously, what would you do as a Twosie or a Threesie? Start a flower shop? You could go to work as a janitor, but you wouldn't be playing golf at Topeka Country Club on a janitor's wages."

"Shit," said Sanjay.

"Shit," said May.

"Yep," said Ron.

Topeka, Kansas
The Topeka Online News Service
September 26, 2077

Breaking News:

In what appears to be a coordinated effort, large crowds of Tier TwoB citizens ransacked FourStores in Baton Rouge, Des Moines, Bismark, Billings, and Atlanta. Many of the rioters were carrying signs that read "Exodus 20:8-11," and most of the people in the crowds were chanting, "Remember the Sabbath Day, to keep it holy."

The rioters broke windows, pulled merchandise from the shelves, trampled on fruits and vegetables, opened boxes of food and scattered the contents on the floors, and smashed chip-reading machines.

Customers in the stores were chased into the streets, and many were hit, spit at, and verbally abused.

Chester Sedgwick, founder and leader of the self-styled "God's Watchdogs," an ultra-conservative Tier TwoB organization, went on television immediately after the hour-long rampages, and took responsibility for the riots.

"What happened back in 2053 was just a warm-up," declared Sedgwick. "These godless commies are going to bring the wrath of almighty God down upon our heads. Doing business on the day the Lord told us to set aside as a day of rest will doom this nation. And make no mistake – if this heathen practice continues, we will destroy every FourStore in the nation. What happened today is just a foretaste."

Neither the Speaker of the Tier TwoB Senate nor any of the Tier Two senators were available for comment.

Topeka, Kansas
The Topeka Online News Service
September 27, 2077

Breaking News:

In several cities across the nation, large crowds of Tier Four citizens have taken to the streets in protest of Tier TwoB attacks on FourStores.

Claiming to be the organizer and leader of the movement, Clarence Richardson of Lansing, Michigan told reporters covering the protests, "We have been trying for over 30 years to get GovOne and GovTwo to do something about their citizens walking around with guns, and they act like they can't even hear us. And now this. Those monsters attacked our peaceful and unarmed citizens because they want to force their religion on everyone else. Well, if the governments won't do anything about it, we're left with no choice. We have to do it ourselves."

Asked what his group plans to do, Richardson replied, "Just you wait and see."

Although no official announcement has been made, it appears that the President has mobilized the National Guard.

Topeka, Kansas
2078

"Tshere's somebody I want you three to meet." Dick was tending to the grill on his patio, and the smell of barbecued ribs was overwhelming. "You ever heard of Sybil Gardner?"

Susannah, newly married and just back from her honeymoon, was sitting with her husband on the glider and holding his hand. They had moved into Susannah's tiny apartment, but had asked Dick to see if he could find them something a little bigger. John O'Reilly was an accountant, and had just joined an accounting firm with offices on Kansas Avenue downtown. *Yarn and Yardage* was doing well, and both of the couple had been able to give up their GMIs. They were proud that they didn't have to take money from their fellow Threesies anymore.

Adam glanced over at Susannah, remembering the times they had talked about getting married. He looked away when Susannah looked over at him.

"I've never heard of her. Have you, Adam?" Susannah didn't want Adam to feel left out. "Mr. O'Reilly, have you heard of her?" She smiled at her husband.

"Why no, Mrs. O'Reilly, I've never heard of her either." John and Susannah giggled.

Dick and Adam rolled their eyes at each other.

"Didn't she write a book? About liberty or something?" Adam asked. "And wasn't there some talk about a bunch of people, mostly Onesies, leaving America to go live on boats? Or islands?"

"Yep, that's the one," Dick replied. "Except I don't think it's boats or islands. I think it's some kind of a floating city. They call it seasteading. You know, like homesteading, except on water. Anyway, Sybil gives talks sometimes. And with me being a Twosie senator and all, I was able to get her to agree to come here and talk to some of us. I've reserved one of the small meeting rooms at the library. She refuses to talk to any group bigger than 20 people, so if you can't be there, or don't want to, let me know so I can invite someone else." He was quiet for a few seconds. "Even if you don't agree with her, even if you're happy with where you are, I think you'll find what she has to say very interesting."

Topeka and Shawnee County Public Library
2078

"So. Who gets to decide?"

Sybil Gardner was 80 years old if she was a day, and she walked with a cane. It was hard to tell whether she needed it for balance, or used it for intimidation. She had probably been taller at one time, but now she was barely five feet. Her eyes were dark brown, and they could be warm. Sometimes. There was nothing unsteady about her voice.

There were ten tables with 20 chairs arranged in a semi-circle. Only 16 of the chairs were filled.

"Okay, I'll ask again. Who gets to decide?"

Some of the group looked down, and some of them frowned in confusion.

"Mr. Maxwell. Who gets to decide?"

Adam's eyes grew wider and his cheeks turned red. How could anyone so old and so short be so intimidating? "I, uh, I don't understand the question. Decide what?"

"Anything. Everything. Who gets to decide things?" Sybil scanned the group. "Susannah. Who gets to make decisions about your life?"

Susannah was determined not to be intimidated. "I guess it depends on what the decision is about."

"Who decides what job you will have?"

"I do."

"Who decides where you will live?"

"I do."

"Who decides whether you will own a gun?"

"The government. My government."

"Who decides where Mr. Maxwell will live?"

"His government."

Sybil scanned the group again, looking for reactions.

"Who decides whether Mr. Carpenter will own a gun?" she continued.

"He does, because he's a Twosie."

"Is this okay with all of you?"

A hand went up.

"Yes, Dr. Patel?"

"It's not okay with me. The government dictating things, I mean."

"Which part? The government dictating things at all, or just the fact that it's different from tier to tier?"

"Uh, well, all of it, I guess. I just don't like them dictating where I live and how much money I can make. "

"So, as a Tier Four doctor, you're unhappy. You'd like more say-so in your life?"

Dr. Patel nodded.

Sybil walked over to Adam again. "Mr. Maxwell, I want you to picture something. Imagine that you can pick out a house for yourself, you can pick a job for yourself, you will be given your full salary in cash, and you can decide what to spend it on and where to shop. You will figure your own taxes, you will decide whether to buy a gun. In short, you will make all the decisions about your own life. What's the first thing you will decide?"

Adam didn't feel very well.

"C'mon, Mr. Maxwell. What's first? Okay, let's narrow it down. Where will you choose to live?"

Adam had never had a panic attack, but he was pretty sure he was having one now.

Sybil put her hand on Adam's shoulder to steady him. "I know we have at least three doctors in the room. Can one of you help Adam put his head between his knees or get him a paper bag to breathe in, or whatever you do in a case like this, and can somebody get him a glass of water please? There's a pitcher and glasses on the table by the door."

While Sanjay and May Wong tended to Adam, Sybil walked back to the middle of the room. She did not apologize to Adam. "I've seen this in a lot of people I talk with, and not just Foursies. I think of it as the Spacewalk Syndrome. Someone described it as the feeling most of us would have if we were asked to make a space walk without a tether, with the infinite universe spread out in front of us. We would have all the liberty in the universe available to us, and we wouldn't be able to handle it. Astronauts love it, but I know I'd throw up in my helmet, because I'm comfortable only here, safely, on earth. And that brings me to my main point."

Sybil walked back to Adam and spoke to him almost gently. "Adam, are you happy with your life as a Foursie? Do you feel safe? Secure? Cared for?"

Adam nodded. "Yes, I do. And that spacewalk thing you talked about—that's exactly what it felt like. You probably don't approve, but I like being a Foursie."

"Why would you think I don't approve? It's not right for me, it's not right for some of the other people in this room right now, but *it's right for you."*

Sybil walked back to the center of the room and leaned on her cane, looking down. The room was very quiet. Finally she looked up. "There are no universal rights and wrongs, with the exception of forcing your beliefs on others. I have no more right to force Mr. Maxwell to live as a Onesie than he has to force me to live as a Foursie. The only question is whether we can all live together.

"As most of you know, there have been groups of people threatening to secede from the United States since, well, before we fought a war about it over 200 years ago, and it's still going on. Over the past two decades, the west coast states have drawn up a number of plans to leave and start a new nation based on socialist principles. There was talk in Texas about being a separate country based on what used to be the Republican Party, and who knows what other states and counties or even cities have wanted to leave. But here's the problem with a geographical area leaving the union. Let's say, for instance that California and Oregon and Washington state seceded and formed the Peoples' Republic of Pacifica. There are a whole big bunch of people in those areas who don't want to live under socialism. They may be in the minority and would probably lose if the matter came to a vote. What do you do with them? Force them to live according to the will of the majority? Any system where 51 percent of the population can force its will on the other 49 percent is headed for trouble. What do you do with all the liberal Texans if their state becomes a separate far-right republic? Buy them out? Force them out?

"The first two decades of this century showed pretty well that we can't all live together peacefully under one government, and President Anderson's well-meaning albeit misguided experiment in all living together under separate governments isn't working, either, as demonstrated by the unrest in the streets and what is almost certainly a looming civil war."

A young African-American man raised his hand.

"Yes, Mr. Jefferson?"

"Are you saying that everyone has to be alike in any given geographical area? Don't you think that diversity is an asset?"

"Racial diversity, religious diversity, cultural diversity, diversity of talent and ability and interests and education and background and outlook are assets to any group of people. It's what keeps us resilient and strong. But true diversity can thrive only where there is tolerance. Let me give you a counterexample. The Tier TwoB that got started here a while back wants to have a tier based solely on fundamentalist Christian beliefs. Breaking any of the Ten Commandments will be a crime. Conducting business on a Sunday will be a crime. I assume you can be a Jew or a Muslim or an atheist and still be a Twobeesie. But you have to *act like* a fundamentalist Christian. That is not tolerance, and because of that, there is no diversity of behavior. And since diversity of behavior isn't tolerated, all the advantages of diversity are lost." Sybil paused a moment, then grinned. "I will give them credit, though – they don't even claim to be diverse. So there's that."

"Now hold on a minute," said an elderly man. "Let's back up a minute. You said that 51 percent of the people can't force their will on the other 49 percent. But isn't that the way a democracy works? Doesn't the majority rule?" His wife, sitting beside him, nodded her agreement.

"Mr. Bridges, I see that both you and your wife Dolores have blue eyes, which puts you in the minority, since there are more brown-eyed people than blue-eyed people in the world. That probably goes for the people in this room as well. How about if this group votes that the blue-eyed people have to give the brown-eyed people all their money?"

"Well, no, you can't do that. I'm pretty sure there's a law against doing something like that."

"I sure hope so," said Dolores.

"If we lived in a democracy where every issue was decided by majority rule, we most certainly could," replied Sybil. "One of the main functions of the American Constitution, at least as it used to be, was to specify exactly what the people, as represented by their elected officials, could vote on. It prevents situations like I just described because Congress can vote only on certain issues.

"So, no, in answer to your question, Mr. Bridges – the majority rules only in matters where people get to vote. And people don't get to vote – or shouldn't get to vote -- on most issues affecting other peoples' lives."

A thin, fashionably-dressed woman in her 40s raised her hand.

"Yes, Ms. Merrill?" Sybil acknowledged her.

"Are you telling us you believe you have the answer? You have an idea for the perfect government?"

Sybil laughed. "Not for a minute. There is no perfect government, and there never will be until there are perfect people. Whatever that means.

"No, I'm saying that a hands-off government with strictly limited powers, a truly free-market economy, and personal liberty that is virtually unlimited as long as you don't take that same freedom away from others, is what's right for me and the people who think like I do.

"We believe that a free-market economy is very much like an ecosystem. Think about a wild meadow with a stream flowing through it and a forest next to it. Think about all the plants, the animals, the insects, the bacteria in the soil. Left alone, it works very well, and evolves to accommodate changes as they occur. A spontaneous order develops. No person or group of people is smart enough to understand everything about it, let alone how to control it. And humanity has proven over and over that no group of people can successfully manipulate an economy. When we try, our happy meadow and forest end up looking like a zoo, with the larger animals in enclosures being fed by humans, the stream dammed up, the trees cut down, and the insects and bacteria gone.

"I realize that some people prefer the zoo, where the animals are guaranteed food, health care, and safety. I prefer the meadow."

Sybil paused and looked around the room to see if there were any more questions.

"So let me tell you why am here, as if you didn't already know.

"A group of us, mostly Onesies, but with a big dose of Twosies and Threesies, and even a smattering of Foursies," -- here she smiled at Adam – "are leaving to start a new nation. My choice for its name is *Libertaria*, but there will be a vote to determine what it will be called. And in the matter of naming the new nation," – Sybil nodded at Don and Dolores – "the majority will rule. Libertaria will be outside the United States territorial waters. Its government will be based partly on the Bylaws of Tier One, partly on the U. S. Constitution as it was originally intended, and partly on new ideas. I am inviting all of you to join us, although I don't recommend it for Adam or anyone else who's happy with the governments you now have here.

"There will be no insurrection, there will be no revolution, there will be no bloodshed. What we are doing is perfectly legal, and we have no desire to bring down any existing government, either here or anywhere else.

"It's true, however, that some of us will never be able to come back, even to visit. If Doctors Wong and Patel and Barry leave with us, they will not have committed a crime. But if they set up a medical practice, and I hope they will, they will immediately be considered criminals under the rules of Tier Four here in the U. S. And if they ever set foot here again, they can be arrested.

"So if any of you are interested in joining us, you would be very welcome. If you'd rather stay here, as I said, no one can tell you

you're wrong. If you're content with your life as it is here, then this is where you belong. And you don't have to let me know. If you want to join us, I can give you contact information."

It was clear that the meeting was over, and the 16 attendees rose. Some headed for the door without a word, but several stayed and gathered into small groups. Adam, Susannah, and John huddled together.

"Sybil's right," said Adam. "I no more belong in Libertaria than I belong on the space station. I'm staying right here."

"We're tempted," said John, "but Susannah's business is doing well, and I like my job. We don't need our GMIs anymore, but the security of knowing they're there if we ever need them is too good to give up."

The three of them nodded politely across the room to Dick and Sybil, who were talking together in the corner, and slipped quietly out the door. They were followed closely by Don and Dolores.

The three doctors and a couple of other attendees approached Sybil and asked for the contact information. When they had left, only Sybil and Raymond Jefferson were left. Raymond stood up, grinning. "Miss Sybil, I want to apply to be the first African-Libertarian."

Libertarian Territorial Waters
January 20, 2079

T he nation of Libertaria consisted of three cruise ships: Libertaria, Tier Zero, and Mayflower Junior. They lay at anchor 207 nautical miles off the coast of southern California, anchored within eyesight of each other and of a small island which would soon be part of their home.

None of the ships was flying an ensign flag, because their citizens had yet to design one. And from the looks of things, it would be a while before that happened. Euphoria was running too high to allow for anything as mundane as designing a national flag.

The previous week, in a display of bravado, several of the citizens of Libertaria – the erstwhile Twosies and Threesies and Foursies, and the handful of Onesies who had been forced to submit to microchip implantation -- had created an impromptu ceremony in which, using razor blades, they removed their own microchips and tossed them overboard. Since the microchips were not deeply implanted, there was more blood than real danger, but it made an impressive, if superficial show. And there was enough gasping and squirming and shuddering from the rest of the citizens to lend gravitas to the occasion.

Although they were probably unaware of it, and had certainly never intended it to be so, their frivolous spectacle served as a substitute for the blood sacrifices – the assassinations, the wars, the atrocities -- that had heretofore always marked and sanctified the founding of new nations.

Most of the rest of the newly-minted Libertarians had their microchips removed by Doctors Wong, Patel, and Barry, who had set up a free-market private practice, with their prices for various procedures clearly displayed. The three doctors were kept busy removing microchips, sewing up incisions, and treating the self-inflicted infections from the previous week.

Two days before, many of the 5,466 citizens of Libertaria had attended, either in person or remotely, a presentation by The Seasteading Institute, a venerable organization founded in 2008 which had been designing sea-based and floating communities for over 60 years. Their sister organization, *Home, Home on the Waves*, would build the floating city which, when anchored to a nearby island and the three ships, would become the permanent home of the Nation of Libertaria.

Now they were settling in to watch the swearing-in of their first president.

Epilogue

"I, Richard Allen Carpenter, do solemnly swear that I will faithfully execute the Office of President of the Nation of Libertaria, and will to the best of my ability, preserve, protect and defend the Constitution of the Nation of Libertaria."

~~~~~~~~~~

"My fellow Libertarians, I cannot express what an honor it is to be the first president of this brand new nation.

"In much of the rest of the world, it is traditional for this speech to be about reunifying the nation after a contentious election, my hopes and plans for the nation, and reassurances that the future is bright. But we are a brand new nation, and we have no such traditions, so I'm not going to waste your time -- and mine -- with platitudes.

"Let's get that out of the way. We don't need reunifying; we're all already pretty much on the same page. My opponents are good people, ran honorable campaigns, and were gracious in defeat. I ask for their support and the support of those who voted for them. You already know what my plans for the future are. Heaven knows I talked about them enough during the campaign. Whether the future is bright will be more your doing than mine, so get to it, okay?

"No, what I want to talk about today isn't addressed so much to you as it is to the vastly larger audience tuned in around the world. For make no mistake, my fellow Libertarians, the world is watching us. And the world needs to hear what I'm about to say more than those of you on these three big boats need to hear it.

"I've been thinking about this for a long time now – maybe longer than some of you have been alive – this idea of government. So let me tell you some of the things I've figured out, some of the things I believe.

"The nuclear family – mother, father, kids – is a natural communist state. The parents have the abilities, the kids have the needs, nobody argues about who has what or who does what or who provides what

or who gets what. The parents willingly provide for their children, and the kids get what they need. That works very well.

"Throw in a couple of grandparents, an elderly aunt or two, and things get complicated pretty fast. Time spent figuring out who gives what and who takes what grows exponentially as the number of people in the group gets bigger.

"A few years back, an anthropologist by the name of Robin Dunbar came up with a number of about 150 as the largest number of friends any one person can have. He said it better than that, something about the largest number of people you can keep track of, and know how they are related to everyone else in the group. 'This is my lawyer's daughter's husband's best friend' sort of thing. The thing is, there's some evidence that 150 was the size of most Neolithic villages and other groups that needed to keep close track of each other, so Mr. Dunbar was probably onto something.

"It's my guess that that's about the largest group you can have where socialism works. If everyone's going to own all the factories and farms and means of distribution collectively, then you'd darn well better be able to know when someone isn't pulling their weight. 'Bill broke his leg and can't help with the turnip harvest. Let's check on him and make sure he's okay, take some food over there for his wife and kids, and call Pete to take his place on the combine. Jerry called to say he's sick and can't make his shift at the factory. But we all know he was drunk all weekend and is probably just hung over. Call him and tell him he won't get his bread ration this week.'

"For any group larger than about 150, the only conceivable system of government is one whose only function is to protect the rights of the citizens, to keep them –and anyone else – from hitting each other, killing each other, or stealing each others' stuff. Period. That's it.

"Now here's the most important thing I'm going to tell you today. If you think you're free because the government gives you more freedom than it gives someone else, think again. The government cannot give *you freedom. You were born with all the freedoms there are just because you were born a human being. The only power a government has is to take away your freedoms. We've all pretty much agreed to let the government take away our freedom to hit, kill, and steal. You get to live your life as you see fit, but when you hit or kill or steal you take away someone else's right to live life as they want to. And that's not okay.*

"Here's something else you need to think about carefully: Any institution that provides you with free food can tell you what and how much food you can have. Any institution that provides you with free housing can tell you where and how you will live. Any institution that provides you with free education can tell you what you will learn, how it will be taught, and what profession you will use it for. And any institution that provides you with free medical care can decide when you are too old or too sick to waste any more medical care on.

"Now, Libertarians, I'm talking to you again. Get out there. Start retail businesses. Grow food. Take care of your families and others close to you. Be a pastor or a rabbi or a priest or an imam. Start voluntary charities to take care of those who can't take care of themselves and have no one else. Make things. Sell things. Be a doctor. Educate children. Be a lawyer. Start factories. Paint pictures. Paint houses.

"I'm ready. Are you?"

STUD FARM

Okay, Danny, Maggie, today is Grampa's 60th birthday, and we're going to go pick him up from the Stud Farm. And as long as we're there we'll be dropping Danny off. So I want you to come over here for a minute and sit down. I just want to make sure you understand what we're doing and why. I know they covered some of this in your history classes, but that's not the same thing as hearing it from someone who was there.

See, along about the second decade of this century, violent crimes just got out of control. It wasn't just robbery and rape – although that was bad enough. I think what finally pushed things over the top was a rash of mass shootings in public places. During one 10-year period several hundred people were killed and over 1500 wounded from nut jobs just walking into public buildings and opening fire. More often than not, it happened at a school, and that just broke peoples' hearts. There were people who were sending exploding packages through the mail. It was about that same time that drones were invented, and a few people figured out how to release poison into the air over crowded cities.

Nobody seemed to be able to say exactly what was causing all the mayhem. As usual, most people blamed it on their pet peeves. A lot of people blamed it on easy access to guns, and another bunch of people said it was because guns were too hard to get and regular citizens couldn't protect themselves. Other people said it was rage, psychosis, depression, other mental illness, bullying, child abuse, alcohol abuse, malnutrition, too many additives in foods, not enough additives in foods, illegal drugs, prescription drugs – including anti-depressants -- poverty, governmental oppression, governmental leniency, parental oppression, parental leniency, parental absence, and I don't know what all else. As near as I can recall, no real link was ever established between the tragedies and any of the causes people were going on and on about. But it didn't matter. People were outraged and frightened and feeling helpless. And outraged, frightened, helpless people are not rational.

Now, here's the deal with people and tragedy. We always feel like, if we just DO SOMETHING, we can fix the problem, or keep it from happening again. Of course, we can almost never agree on just exactly what it is we should do, but we should DO SOMETHING. Figure out the cause of the problem, eliminate the causes, and you're done, right? Except no two people could agree on what the causes were.

In the meantime, relations between different countries were falling apart. National leaders – just about all of them men -- brought the world close to nuclear war more than once, and the reasons for the bickering were never clear. They blamed each other for imposing unfair tariffs, threatening each others' sovereign territory, dumping immigrants across borders, trying to keep immigrants from crossing borders, building weapons in defiance of treaties, imposing sanctions, imposing tariffs, and any number of other real and not-so-real crimes.

The tipping point came during the State of the Union speech in January 2025. The nation was more tense than anyone had ever seen it, and I think we were all looking to the President for help in saving our country and maybe even the world. Instead, the Leader of the Free World started in pontificating on how wonderful everything was going to be under his new administration and how deranged, impotent, and incompetent the leaders of the other nations – all of them men – were. It wasn't what anybody wanted to hear, and most everybody watching the speech was appalled. And frightened. Senator Marge Russell stood up and yelled out what everyone was thinking: "Oh, for God's sake! Just drop your pants, I'll go get a ruler, and we'll settle this once and for all!"

The Secret Service started toward Senator Marge to escort her out of the room, just as Senator Karen Gaither jumped up and yelled, "I've got a better idea. Let's just put all of 'em away somewhere where they can't hurt anyone and we'll finally have some peace!"

The entire room burst into applause and cheers, and most of the crowd started toward the podium. The Secret Service changed course, grabbed the President, and got him out of the room. It was two weeks before anyone saw him in public again. By that time the newly-elected Vice President, Mildred Burch, had taken over. The President had the good sense to resign, but it wouldn't have mattered if he had tried to keep his office. Within a month he was marched off to an internment center along with a little over a third of the rest of the nation.

See, right after that aborted State of the Union speech, before the evening was over, as a matter of fact, people started posting on line about how 60 percent or 74 percent or 95 percent or 112 percent of all violent crimes are committed by young-to-middle-aged men. And the crimes committed by women are usually about some man or involve some man or are instigated by some man.

I do believe that Congress has never acted so fast in the history of this nation. Within a month a law was passed that all males between the ages of 15 and 60 would be placed in internment camps or holding centers. One of the reasons the Congress was able to get that law passed was that 20 percent of the legislators were women and a big chunk of the men legislators were too old to be affected by it. And they were showing the nation that they were DOING SOMETHING.

Of course there were a bunch of people running around arguing about how the mass incarceration of one out of every three people in the nation was unconstitutional. They were quoting Benjamin Franklin when he talked about how if you give up liberty to buy safety, you don't deserve either liberty or safety. But most people were so tired and so scared all the time that they didn't care. We were finally DOING SOMETHING.

A lot of people were complaining about how you can't put people behind bars if they haven't been convicted of a crime, but others were saying how we did that to the Japanese-Americans during World War II, so there was a precedent. There were other precedents, too. Some years before, a trend had started where legislators decided that the most efficient way to stop crime is to prevent crime. They began to criminalize, not the crime, but the possibility of a crime. You might shoot someone, so you were not allowed to own a gun. You could be arrested, not because you shot someone, but because there was a possibility that you would shoot someone. You might take a drink, so you were not allowed to carry an open bottle of liquor in your car. You could be arrested, not for driving drunk, but because there was an opportunity for you to drive drunk.

What with that mindset firmly in place, the next step was easy. If you were a young-to-middle-aged man, you could be incarcerated, not because you had committed a violent crime, but because there was a higher probability of you committing a violent crime.

So, even though the libertarian-thinking minority were pretty upset about what was happening, the majority thought that it was at least worth a try.

And here's the thing: it worked. After everything kind of got settled down, the rate of violent crime dropped to almost nothing, and it has stayed that way ever since. That's probably the main reason nobody has thought seriously about reversing the decision.

Now, since most of the men hadn't actually done anything wrong, the women decided that the men in the penitentiaries should be treated really nice. They weren't being punished, after all. It was more a kind of preventive incarceration.

I was pregnant with your Uncle Kevin that year. Since your Grampa was 24 years old, he was marched off to the pen along with the rest of them, and I really missed him for a while. It was especially hard when Kevin was born and there was no man around to help out. There were a lot of women in the same boat, of course, and women have historically been inclined to believe the old adage that it takes a village to raise a child. It wasn't more than a couple of years before there were free day-care centers in every city. Within five years the nation was, in effect, socialist. There was free health care, free education through college, a high minimum wage, guaranteed jobs, and crippling taxes high enough to pay for all those services AND to pay to keep all those men in jail. But that's the price of guaranteed safety, right?

Now, I'm not saying that a government run entirely by women and old men doesn't have its own set of problems. Most of the time our legislative sessions look like an episode of "The Real Housewives of the Geriatric Ward." But at least there's no violence.

When we first talked about sending the men away, some people said we should just castrate them and keep them around. But that created the same problem as total separation of the sexes – namely that the human race would last only another 100 years. So a system was set up that a woman who wanted children could do one of two things: she could visit an inmate of her choice and get pregnant the old-fashioned way, or she could be artificially inseminated with the sperm of the inmate of her choice. I went to visit your Grampa a lot right at first, and that's how I got Rachel, your mother.

That has set up a lot of competition among the inmates, of course. In order to be the "inmate of choice" for as many women as possible, most of the younger ones keep themselves healthy and fit. A lot of them even put ads on line with their pictures and qualifications as good sperm donors. When we first sent the men off, the incarceration centers were called "Men Pens." But it wasn't long before some women got to calling them "Stud Farms," and the name stuck.

Now, it's true that technology has made it so that women can do just about any job that needs doing, even without a lot of physical strength, but there's one field that has never caught on as well when women do it, and that's sports. Yes, I know there are women's teams in just about every sport, but nobody cares very much. They never have, and they probably never will. So the different stud farms organized themselves some pretty impressive teams – football and baseball and soccer and basketball and I don't know what all else. They all have names just like college and professional teams used to, like the Leavenworth Lions, the Terre Haute Terrors, the San Quentin Squires, the Seastead Buccaneers. They have leagues and almost all the games are televised.

So, pretty much, all the young-to-middle-aged men in this country sit around watching sports, having occasional sex, and asking someone to bring 'em a sandwich. And that suits a lot of 'em just fine.

And since today is Grampa's 60th birthday, we get to go pick him up and bring him home. And, Danny, since you turned 14 a couple of months ago, we need to drop you off at the farm before you turn 15. Since we're making the trip anyway, this seems like as good a time as any.

But don't you worry. It won't be so bad.

STINSON

My name is George Dawson. I was born in 1808. It's 1959 now, and I'm pretty sure I'm 88 years old.

I'm sitting here waiting for the next wagon to come through.

~~~~~~

It was easiest for the first few who came through. Hell, as near as anyone can figure, when old Jedediah Stinson and his family came through first, just a few minutes had passed. But it did get a lot harder for the later arrivals, and I can't imagine what it's going to be like for the ones yet to come.

If there are any.

~~~~~~

Our wagon train was 17 days west of Independence, Missouri, and we were in the heart of Kansas Territory. We had left Independence May 16, 1835. I've heard that by the 1850s the traffic on the Santa Fe Trail was pretty much, as they say now, bumper to bumper. For us, it wasn't that crowded yet, and our ten wagons and 35 people hadn't had any company after the trading post at Council Grove.

That night we had camped just east of an easy ford on a small river. The river was wide right there, and the water was clear, cold, and shallow. The banks on either side wouldn't be a problem for the animals or the wagons either going into the water or coming up the other side. We men-folk watered and fed the oxen and horses while the women built the fires and cooked dinner. We had managed to bring down a good-sized deer that morning, and a little fresh venison was a welcome addition to our usual dinner of dried beans, bacon, hardtack, and parched corn. By sunset everyone was asleep.

You'd have to go a long way to find a prettier sight than a spring morning on the prairie. When we broke camp at daybreak, the skies were as clear a blue as you'll ever see, and the air was cool enough that the rising sun was bringing up a heavy mist off the river. That mist was so thick you couldn't see the opposite bank.

We were eager to get moving, so we ate what was left from dinner the night before, drank some coffee, filled up the water barrels, and lined up the wagons. Sarah's and my wagon was the fourth in line. Old Jedediah was first. He had organized the train and was the acknowledged leader of the group. Often as not, his wife Rachel drove the oxen while Jed and their grown sons Tom and Matt walked alongside. They had a daughter, Martha, too – as pretty a girl as you'd ever want to meet. When Rachel drove the wagon, Martha would sit up there beside her ma. Along with being the leader of the train, Jed was the oldest. I'm guessing he was well past 40. Wagon train travel is a young man's endeavor, but Jed was smart and tough. He had almost no schooling, but what he didn't know about farming and wagons and livestock wasn't worth knowing. He was a pretty fair blacksmith, too.

Anyway, Jed looked back to see that all ten wagons were in place, climbed up into the driver's seat, and moved off toward the river. They eased down the bank on the east side and into the mist hanging over the river.

That was the last time I ever saw Jedediah Stinson or any of his family. Well, except for his great- and great-great grandkids. But

I'm coming to that.

~~~~~~

Now, I wasn't there to see it. But from my own experience and from stories handed down by those who came through later, I can pretty well guess what happened next. The ford was shallow enough for a man to walk across, so Jed had his sons walk a little ahead, one on either side, to watch for dangerous rocks. Jed, with his wife beside him and his daughter in the back of the wagon, was concentrating on getting his family and all their belongings safely across that river and up the other bank. It was slow going, especially with that heavy mist, but pretty soon the oxen started laboring up the shallow bank on the west side and they left the water behind. They got out of the mist and went on a couple hundred yards to leave space for the wagons coming right behind. Jed handed the reins to Rachel so he could walk back and see if anyone was having trouble getting across. Moses and Mazie were next in line, then the Wills brothers, Jake and Jesse. Jed wasn't worried about any of them. Moses could handle a team of oxen better than Jed could, and the Wills boys were young bachelors with no women-folk with them. But some of the others might need some help.

Jed got down off the wagon and turned to walk back. All he saw was empty trail. He told his sons to stay with the women and walked back toward the river to see if Moses was having a problem. And when he got close to the river, there was no mist. He walked back across the river, past our camping place of the night before, climbed the small hill just a bit farther east, and looked out across several miles of empty prairie.

There was no possibility his entire wagon train could have turned around and driven out of sight that fast. If we had been attacked by hostile Indians or robbers, he would have heard the commotion and seen the carnage.

Jedediah had no idea what to do. Going back east didn't make any sense, since he could see further back down the trail than a wagon train could have travelled in an hour. And he didn't feel like he could go on toward Santa Fe, just in case we showed up again somehow.

Since he didn't know the right thing to do, he didn't do much of anything for a while. He pulled his wagon over onto a grassy spot and waited. He waited the rest of that day, and the next day, too. He probably began to wonder if all the rest of us, along with our livestock, our wagons, and all our gear had been raptured right up into heaven, and he and his family had been left behind.

On the third day, another wagon train came across the river. Jed asked them if they had seen nine wagons headed back toward Independence, and he gave a pretty fair description of all of us. None of the strangers had seen so much as a lone rider headed east. The strangers asked if the Stinsons wanted to join their train, but Jed and his family decided they'd just stay put for a while.

It would be 25 years before they knew what had happened.

That summer Jed and his sons built a sod house and dug a well and a root cellar, and the family planted a vegetable garden with some seeds Rachel had brought along for her first garden in Santa Fe. The weather was good to them and the garden did well in the virgin soil. The men hunted pheasants, quail, deer, and rabbits, and by the end of the summer the Stinson family had stored up a good supply of dried meats and root vegetables.

Of course, the wagon trains kept coming through, and the Stinsons often traded some of their fresh vegetables for flour so Rachel and Martha could keep the family supplied with bread.

Late that fall, a wagon train that had made a late start got caught in a snowstorm and decided to spend the winter camped across the trail from the Stinson homestead. Martha took quite a liking to the young son of the train leader, so when the weather cleared in the spring of 1836, Martha went with them. It just about broke

Rachel's heart, but she and Jed understood that living out on the prairie with just her ma and pa and brothers was not the way a pretty young girl was supposed to live. Before they left, Jed got a solemn promise from the young man's father that Martha and her beau would be properly married as soon as they reached Santa Fe.

One of the families in that wagon train had bought a poorly made wagon which had given them nothing but trouble since they had started out. It was plain to see they weren't going to make it to Santa Fe in that wagon, nor back to Independence either, so they decided to stay where they were. Jed traded them some dried meat and a supply of turnips for half a sack of wheat seed.

During that first winter, Jed built a forge. The next spring he and his sons built two more small houses so Tom and Matt, who were 25 and 22 by that time, could each have their own place. They planted a bigger garden and a good sized wheat field.

By the summer of 1836, the town of Stinson, Kansas Territory, had about a dozen people living there, and they were able to offer fresh vegetables, fresh game, and blacksmith services to the travelers in exchange for bullets, cloth, and about anything else they couldn't make for themselves.

By 1860, the town of Stinson had a population of several hundred. Jed and Rachel had replaced their old sod hut with a nice stone house as soon as it was pretty obvious they were going to stay. It had a porch, and Jed and Rachel liked to sit out there in a pair of rockers Jed had made. Old Jedediah was coming up on 70 years of age. Rachel was 67 and was ailing pretty badly with rheumatism, but both their sons had married local girls and the boys and their wives and children were doing a good job of taking care of the farming and the blacksmith shop and the trading post. Jed and Rachel had grown grandkids and a few great-grandkids by then, and were trying to take it easy.

One warm spring morning that year Jed came out his front door figuring to sit on his porch for a while and see what traffic there was. He looked east toward the sunrise.

And here came Moses and Mazie, the second in line in our wagon train, climbing up the bank of the river in their covered wagon. Their sons Abraham and Aaron were walking alongside.

~~~~~~

Moses was a runaway slave from Kentucky, a big, strapping man not much younger than Jed. There had been quite a bit of opposition to his joining the wagon train, on account of his color, but Jedediah said anyone of his size who had the strength and courage to escape from slavery would be a real asset to our group. Jed put him second in line. Jed knew Moses would be able to get his own wagon through just about anything, and then walk back and help anyone who was having trouble.

I don't think I ever met a man with as little to say as Moses. His wife, Mazie, was shy and a little standoffish, but after the women-folk got to know her, she filled them in on some of their history. Moses hardly ever said much of anything – he just worked. Some of the men, and even a couple of the women, right at first, called him "boy." Or worse. Moses would just look them in the eye with no expression on his face and no words coming out of his mouth. If anyone looked like they were going to cause trouble for Moses' wife or sons, he'd just walk over and stand quietly between his family and the troublemaker and stare them down.

Then one evening, just a week or ten days out of Independence, we camped early by a river with a nice pool just right for bathing. The men tended the camp while the women bathed and washed their hair and their clothes. Then the men went down to bathe. We all stripped naked and waded into that cold water. That's when we all got a look at Moses' body. That man had scars from his neck to his feet, front and back. I didn't see how anyone could have been whipped like that and lived to tell about it.

We shouldn't have stared like that, but it was hard to look away.

Finally, in the silence, Jed asked, "Moses, what in hell happened to you?"

Moses was quiet for a minute, then he said, "I escaped that plantation three times. The first two times, they dragged me back and beat me so bad I was in bed for a month. The third time I escaped, I took a knife and swore I'd slit my own throat before I'd go back. But that time I made it."

We finished our baths in silence, and I never heard anyone call Moses "boy" again. And I never heard Moses speak more than three or four words together again.

Of course, the men told their women about what they had seen and heard, and it seemed to me the women were friendlier toward Mazie after that. Part of it was compassion, but a lot of it was curiosity. My Sarah told me the rest of the story Mazie had told the women.

After his escape, Moses made his way north, and ended up in Ohio.

Mazie had never known what it was to be a slave. Her father, Simon, and his family had belonged to a plantation owner in Alabama. But ol' Massah Hodges, as Simon called him, had put it in his will that all his slaves were to be given their freedom when he died. That happened when Simon was a small boy, and his family went north. Simon became a successful businessman, and saw to it that his children received a good education.

The day Moses applied for a job in Simon's warehouse, Mazie was helping in the office. Moses had no formal education, since schooling was usually forbidden to slaves, but there was no harder worker to be found at any wage. Mazie offered to teach him to read and write. By the time Moses could form his letters well, they were planning their wedding. By the time he was reading textbooks, they had two sons.

By 1835, the boys were in their late teens, the family had saved some money, and they decided to head for Santa Fe.

~~~~~~

It's likely, on that spring morning in 1860, that Moses and Mazie wouldn't have even recognized Jedediah. After all, from their viewpoint, they had followed Jed and his family into that mist about five minutes ago, with eight more wagons right behind them. And here they were coming up the other bank of the river, into a town where there hadn't been a town the night before, and here was a 70-year-old man coming off his porch and hobbling toward them as fast as he could. He looked sort of like someone they ought to know, but they couldn't quite place him. He kept looking behind them to see if there were more wagons, but the road clear to the river, and beyond, was empty.

Old Jedediah stood there for a full minute with his jaw just going up and down, and finally yelled, "Where in hell have you BEEN?"

Of course, Moses and Mazie looked just like Jed remembered them. They had aged about half an hour since he last saw them.

I can't imagine what the rest of that day was like for those two families. They must have sat at the kitchen table in that Stinson homestead and talked for hours trying to puzzle out what had happened. I doubt they ever got their questions answered, but it was about that time they realized that if there were more wagons coming through, somebody had to be there to meet them. The world had changed a lot in the 25 years Jed and Rachel had been there. If it was another 25 years before another family came through, Lord only knew what sights would greet them. Somebody had to be there to help the next wagon.

So Moses and his family settled in and built a farm just a little upstream from Jed and Rachel. The year after that, Kansas entered the union as a free state, and the Civil War started.

Abraham was 19 and Aaron was 17 when the war started, and both boys wanted to join up. The army wasn't supposed to take anyone under 18, but Aaron lied about his age and was allowed to be a drummer boy.

One of the problems was that the family had no last name. It was common for slaves to assume the last name of their master, but Moses would have none of that. He had spent many years, defiantly, without a last name, but his sons could not sign up for the Union army without one.

Moses went to Jedediah and asked, since Jed had always treated him and his family decently, if Jed would mind if Moses' family took Jed's last name. Jed said he thought that was a fine idea. After that the town of Stinson had a white Stinson family and a black Stinson family. And Abraham Stinson and Aaron Stinson marched off to war.

Abraham was killed in battle in 1864. He was 22 years old.

Aaron came home at the end of the war, but he was restless and impatient. The war and the death of his brother had been hard on him, and there were no marriage prospects for him in Stinson. Mazie died in 1879, and it seemed to be what Aaron was waiting for. A couple of years before that, the town of Nicodemus had been founded up in Northern Kansas. It was a town built by and for former slaves. Mazie was in her grave barely two weeks before Aaron took off. Moses wasn't too happy about it, but I'm sure he understood.

I hope Aaron did well.

It wasn't too long after the war ended that Jake and Jesse Wills came through. Jake and Jesse were young bachelors and the second and third sons of a wealthy landowner in Missouri. Their father had refused to divide his land among his three sons, so Jake and Jesse took their share of their father's wealth in cash and headed west. When they came through in 1867, Jed, Moses, Mazie, and Aaron were there to meet them. Rachel had died in 1864.

By then they were pretty certain that the wagons were coming through in the order they crossed the river, so they knew Sarah and I would be next. It also looked like the ones who came through did so about daybreak, and always in the spring. But the timing was unpredictable, and they all agreed that someone needed to be there for Sarah and me when we got there.

When Sarah and I came through in 1898, the only one we had known before was Jesse Wills, and he was 51 years old. Jed, Moses, and Mazie were all buried in a pretty little hilltop cemetery up back of the Stinson homestead, along with Rachel, Tom, Matt, and Jake Wills, who had died in a runaway horse accident the year before.

Sarah and I were newlyweds, 20 and 27 years old, but as young and strong as we were, I don't know how we would have handled what we saw. By then, Stinson had a train depot about half a mile west of the river, and there was a train coming into the station just as we came out of the mist. The whistle was blowing and the smoke was pouring out, and Sarah started screaming. I couldn't help her because I was darn near as scared as she was. By then Jesse Wills had run up to our wagon and was yelling, "It's all right! It's okay! Don't be scared! It won't hurt you!" It didn't calm us down much, coming from a man who had aged over 30 years in the half hour since we had seen him.

Jesse managed to lead our horses over close to the Stinson homestead and help Sarah down from the wagon. He and one of Jed Stinson's great-grandsons got her inside and calmed down a bit. I wasn't much help since I was shaking so bad I could barely walk. So we sat there with Jesse while he filled us in on what was going on, or at least as much of it as he and the others had been able to figure out.

The Santa Fe Trail didn't exist any more. The railroad had taken care of that, so it didn't make any sense for Sarah and me to keep traveling west in a world that we couldn't figure out and where we didn't fit. Besides, Jesse and Sarah and I were the only ones left, and Jesse was aging. Somebody had to stay to meet the rest of the wagon train. There were descendents of the original travelers, of course, but a lot of them had moved away. And most of the ones who had stayed didn't even believe the stories we told.

John and Mary Olson and their baby girl Rose came through in 1931. By then I was the only one to meet them. The old place where we had all climbed up out of that river wasn't on any kind of a road any more. A few years before, they had built some fancy roads, and the fancy new roads needed fancy bridges over rivers and streams and gullies and such. The new road ran a mile or two downstream of our crossing, which was a good thing. If it had been built where we crossed, when John and Mary came up that bank their heads would have been just about where the base of the bridge was. I hate to think what that would have meant.

You may have noticed that a lot of our group lived longer than you would have expected for their time. I don't know if it's just because we were tougher than average or if coming through that mist did something to us, but my Sarah wasn't that lucky. She died in 1907 giving birth to our first child. The baby died with her. It was the worst thing that's ever happened to me.

In 1925 the town of Stinson opened a public library. I have some education and had planned to start a newspaper when we got to Santa Fe, so I enjoy that library. I read a lot of history.

In 1935 the government started up this program called Social Security. You have to fill in a lot of forms and such, and you're supposed to have a birth certificate. It wasn't much of a problem right then. After all, in 1935 there were a lot of people who didn't have birth certificates. I don't know how the rest of the people yet to come through are going to handle that.

About 1950 or so, Mary Olson and Rose made a trip to Dodge City and came back all excited. They had visited a fancy store where they sold old things, and sold them for a lot of money. They called them antiques. Mary said the old washing boards and butter churns and lamps and tools and dishes and silverware were in demand. Of course, the Stinson homestead had an attic and a couple other rooms full of that stuff that had been brand new when our wagon train started out. The things that had belonged to the two Stinson families had been used a lot, and really looked as old as they were. But the things that were mine and Sarah's and the Olsons' were still pretty new. So we rebuilt the store that had been the old Stinson Trading Post and renamed it Stinson Antiques. We set out some of the things from the attic and back rooms. Turns out that coins dated 1832 or 1833 in almost new condition – well, let's just say the Olsons and I are taking it easy and leaving the farming to the younger folks.

Since my primary function these days is to look for more people coming through, I've done a lot of thinking about it. There's no guarantee there will be any more wagons. Maybe after the first five, the mist just cleared up and the rest of them crossed the river, tried to figure out where the first five wagons had gone, scratched their heads for a while, and went on to Santa Fe. In my history readings I've tried to find mention of people out west with their family names, but haven't come up with anything definite.

I even thought about going to Santa Fe and looking up people named Wallace and O'Connor and Brandon and Schilling and Brown. But what would I do if I found them? Walk up to their door and knock and say, "Excuse me, do you have any family stories about your great-great-great-great-grandfather coming west in a covered wagon and losing half of the wagons in the mist? If so, I was in that wagon train and I knew him!" I about laughed myself silly thinking about explaining that to the police while they were dragging me away.

In any case, I don't dare leave Stinson. Especially about daybreak in the spring. Somebody has to be here to explain electricity and running water and flush toilets and televisions and radios and cars and airplanes and women with shaved legs.

~~~~~~

My name is George Dawson. I was born in 1808. It's 1959 now, and I'm pretty sure I'm 88 years old.

I'm sitting here waiting for the next wagon to come through.

If there are any.

THE CLEANSING

The gates Vincent found himself in front of did, in fact, have a kind of pearly shine to them. The soft sound coming from behind them, while not exactly music, had hints of mothers singing and summer breezes and laughter and babies cooing and gentle words spoken between lovers. Vincent knew there was no place he wanted to be more than he wanted to be behind those gates.

Vincent became aware of someone standing beside him. Turning, he saw a tall, bearded man in a white robe. He had a leather belt from which hung a set of very old keys. He looked remarkably like the pictures thumb tacked to the bulletin board in Vincent's third-grade Sunday school room.

"Are you Saint Peter?" asked Vincent.

"That's the way you see me," said the man, "because that's what you expected. In fact, this is my 21st- Century Midwestern American Conservative Protestant look and voice. People who come from other backgrounds and faiths see and hear me very differently. And some people don't see me at all because their faith traditions don't include a gatekeeper for paradise."

"Can you let me in there?' asked Vincent, gesturing at the Pearly Gates. " I really want to get in there."

"Oh, I can't let you in there, Vincent. Contrary to legend, I don't decide who goes in and when. You will let yourself in when the time comes. But that time hasn't come yet, Vincent, not yet," answered Peter. "You've got some work to do first."

"I thought all the work I needed to do came before I died," said Vincent. "I joined a church. I gave to charity. I don't have a body any more. I don't see what kind of work you expect from me."

"Well, Vincent, welcome to Purgatory."

~~~~~~~

"Purgatory? How can I be in Purgatory? I'm not Catholic. Only Catholics go to Purgatory!" Vincent was almost yelling.

Peter seemed not to hear him. "Let me introduce you to your guide, Vincent. Or rather, let me bring your guide to you, since you've met him before. Eddy will show you around, explain how this works, answer all your questions, and get you set up at your own station." Peter lifted one of the keys hanging from his belt and pointed it at the gates.

The gates didn't open so much as they became translucent. The joyous noises from inside became just a little louder, and Vincent thought he could detect a faint smell of flowers and new crayons and fresh-baked biscuits and the way babies smell when they've just been bathed. He thought he caught a whiff of the baby blanket his mother had knit for him, the blanket that always made him feel safe and loved. Up until that moment he hadn't known the blanket had a smell, but now it filled him with peace and security and joy. The light inside the gates was soft and inviting and warm. Vincent wanted to run inside, but he knew he wouldn't get in yet. He had some work to do.

There was a figure coming toward him through the gates, and Vincent recognized him immediately. His heart sank. "Eddy? You're my guide? Oh my God, I mean oh my gosh, I'm so glad you're in heaven. Not that I doubted for a minute that you'd get here, of course, but you look exactly the same! I mean, that's okay, of course, but I guess I expected something different, some improvement. You've still got that scar on your forehead where we...and your eyes are still kind of slanty... and..."

Vincent stopped blathering. Eddy was standing calmly with his hands crossed in front of him, a slight and kindly smile on his lips.

"They're called epicanthal folds, Vincent. I had Down Syndrome in life, and right now I look the way I did in life for your sake, so you can remember and do the work you need to do."

"You mean, in there," Vincent gestured toward the gates, "you look bett... different?"

"In there," said Eddy," I am the perfect, shining soul I always was inside, the part of me you were never able to see." Vincent suddenly realized that there was not a trace of the speech impediment he and his friends had so cruelly mocked.

Eddy turned to Peter. "Thank you, Peter. I think Vincent and I can take it from here." As Peter walked (floated? soared?) away, Vincent wasn't surprised to see that Peter's robe was now blue, he had acquired a yellow cloak, and his keys now hung from a cord around his wrist. He looked exactly like the El Greco painting.

~~~~~~~

Eddy started to move away to his left and gestured for Vincent to come along with him. Vincent stayed where he was. He dreaded being alone with Eddy. The shame of his past behavior was overwhelming, and he couldn't think of anything to say to avoid the subject.

Eddy stopped and looked back. "Vincent, you need to come with me. I have a lot of things to explain to you, a lot of things to show you. I'm sure you have questions, too, and I am glad to answer them for you. For example, most newly-arrived people want to know how they can still have so many physical sensations when they no longer have a body."

"I was wondering about that," said Vincent.

"The answer is that you are still so closely tied to earth that you need the sensation of having a physical existence in order not to become disoriented. And the work you are going to do requires you to retain the capability for all the emotions you had in life. Once you have completed your work, sadness, anger, fear, hatred, jealousy will all be in the past. But right now, you still need them."

Eddy started forward again, and Vincent fell in step beside him. Eddy continued, "You will find that your sense of time is exactly as it was in life. There is no day or night here, you won't need to sleep, you will not eat or drink because you will feel neither hunger nor thirst, but the passage of time will not change from the way you experienced it before."

"How about in there?" asked Vincent, pointing back at the Pearly Gates.

"Oh, in there, it's not...," Eddy paused for a moment, thinking, "...it's not that the concept of time doesn't exist. There are many opportunities for continued spiritual growth, and growth implies the passage of time. It's more that the concept of time is irrelevant. Never-ending joy is outside the bounds of time."

Vincent felt emboldened. "Say, Eddy, about that time Jerry and Tony and I, you know, were kind of mean to you, well, hey, I was just a kid, you know? We were all just kids. We didn't really mean it, you know? Not really, anyway."

"You were a kid, yes," replied Eddy. "But you were old enough to decide to be cruel. And that makes you responsible for what you did."

That was not the answer Vincent had hoped for.

"Yeah, well, okay. I'm sorry, and I hope you forgive me."

"Oh, Vincent. I forgave you a long time ago."

"Thanks, Eddy. So we're okay then?"

"There are two kinds of forgiveness, Vincent. When I forgave you, it was for my own sake. As they say, hatred is like an acid. It does as much harm to the vessel it's stored in as it does to the object it's poured on. I forgave you so that I wouldn't be carrying around the anger, the fear, the hatred that was weighing down my own soul. But here's what you need to understand, Vincent. That forgiveness didn't do *you* any good because *you* didn't participate. You have never actually asked for my forgiveness."

"I thought that was what I just did."

"What? That offhand remark? Hardly! Here, Vincent, take hold of my hand."

Vincent reluctantly touched his fingers to the hand Eddy had extended. Suddenly, he was 11 years old again. He was laughing and running across a vacant lot toward three boys, although his running was more labored than he remembered. He was happy to see the boys because he knew them from the neighborhood and hoped they would be his friends. When Vincent suddenly realized one of the three boys was himself, he understood that the mind of the body he was in was different from his. He was the 11-year-old Eddy.

Jerry yelled to Vincent and Tony, "Hey, guys, look! It's the Mongoloid!" He pulled the corners of his eyes up with his fingers. "Ching, Ching, Ching. Hey, you, can you even talk yet?"

Eddy had stopped running. He stood there, confused and hurt. Vincent felt every pang.

He saw himself pick up a rock and throw it, hard. "Get out of here, you ree-tard! Nobody wants you around here!" The rock hit Eddy above his right eye, opening a cut that poured blood down his face, and would leave a scar he would carry the rest of his short life.

Eddy collapsed to the ground, dazed, scared, hurt, sobbing, and wiping at the blood pouring from the cut. The three boys ran away, laughing, leaving Eddy there alone.

Vincent returned to his own body.

"Oh, Eddy! I am so sorry!" Vincent was curled on the ground at Eddy's feet, in exactly the same position Eddy had been all those years ago. "I don't know what to say!" he sobbed." There's no excuse! Please, please forgive me!"

"Now, that's an apology!" said Eddy. "Yes, Vincent, you are forgiven."

Eddy helped Vincent to his feet. "By the way, 'You are forgiven' is very different from 'I forgive you'. The Creator has now forgiven you because you actually felt the harm you had done and were truly sorry."

"But it didn't fix anything," said Vincent. "You were still damaged for the rest of your life." He was still weeping, and Eddy made no effort to stop him or comfort him.

"That's true," replied Eddy. "Wise people have known for a long time that the damage done by intentional cruelty can't be undone any more than I could get rid of the scar that rock you threw gave me. If you intentionally hurt another creature, all you can do is try to understand what they have felt, repent, and accept the gift of forgiveness with gratitude, joy, and humility."

They moved in silence for a while.

"You know, Eddy, after we grew up I really thought about getting hold of you to apologize."

"That would have been nice, Vincent."

"I don't know, I just never got around to it. I wasn't sure if you still lived where you did when you were a kid. And there just always seemed to be something else to take care of. You know how it is, right?"

Eddy didn't answer.

"And I was ashamed. I didn't know what to say."

Eddy still didn't answer.

"And then you died."

"I died at 42 of pneumonia," said Eddy. "Back then that was a pretty long life for someone with Down Syndrome."

"So I guess I thought that was the end of it. There wasn't anything I could do after that," continued Vincent.

Eddy stopped and turned to face Vincent. "You could have asked God for forgiveness. By then I had already rid my soul of the fear and hatred you had caused, but The Father would have forgiven you, and you would have been free of the guilt you carried for all those years. And I would have known and been glad. You would have had one fewer job to do here in Purgatory."

"Can I just say one more thing about this, Eddy? I accept the blame for what I did. And I'm more grateful that I can say that I don't have to deal with that any more. But you do know, don't you, that my father was one mean old son-of-a-bitch. Most of what I learned about how to be cruel I learned from him. Do you know what happened when I got home that day? I bragged to him about what Jerry and Tony and I had done to you, and he laughed! He clapped me on the back and told me I had done a good job."

"Yes, I know that, Vincent. When your father arrived here, I was one of the souls he had to deal with in the same way you had to deal with me. So let's go talk with him."

"My father? He's here?"

"Of course he's here, Vincent. He's working very hard, just as you will have to do."

"No! I don't want to see him or talk with him. I avoided him the last 20 years of his life and I was glad when he died. There's no reason for me to see him now!"

"Think about what I told you before, Vincent. Your fear of and hatred for your father are weighing you down. For your soul's sake, you need to get rid of that burden. But for your father's sake, you must give him a chance to ask your forgiveness."

"I don't want to see him! I don't want to talk to him!" Vincent paused and thought quietly for a minute. "You mean to tell me that if I don't forgive him, he can't get into heaven? Sounds pretty good to me."

"Oh, he can get in, Vincent. Your refusal to see him doesn't diminish the fact that he's eager to see you and will do everything he can to heal your relationship. It's his effort that counts. But your refusal to participate will damage you without hurting him at all."

~~~~~~~

As they approached the figure standing waiting for them, Vincent thought his father looked, not so much smaller, but somehow *diminished*. In life, Vincent's father had been a hulking man who seemed even bigger because of his belligerent attitude. But now the swagger, the bluster, the defiance, were gone. They had been replaced by a look of calm acceptance and something that looked a lot like humility. He acknowledged Eddy's presence with a nod and a friendly smile, and Eddy returned the gesture. Vincent's father turned to his son.

"Vincent, I am so glad to see you! You don't know how hard it's been for me to wait here for you all these years. I know you don't want to be here with me, and I don't blame you. But I hope you will listen to what I have to say. In the years since I died I have met with all the people I hurt in life who had come here before me, and we are all reconciled. Now I have to wait here at my station to meet with the people who died after I did. If I had made an effort to ask their forgiveness when we were all still alive, I wouldn't have had to spend all these years here at my station. Who knows? I might already have made it through those gates." He smiled ruefully.

"Vincent, you and your mother and your little brother are the ones I have dreaded meeting the most, because I hurt you the most. Like you, I had a pretty terrible childhood, and it turned me into a pretty terrible person. But I take the responsibility for what I did and the choices I made. Your mother, God rest her soul – Literally, Vincent! – she's in there, at peace, and really happy – she forgave me right away. It didn't take her long to go through the gates. I bet she didn't hurt a dozen people in her whole life, and when she did hurt someone, she made amends right away, so she didn't have much work to do."

Without being asked, Vincent reached out and took his father's hand. It all came flooding back. He watched his father curse his mother and push her up against the wall. He felt his father shove five-year-old Vincent's face into his birthday cake because he was drunk and he thought it would be funny. He sat through every dinner, listening to his father berate his mother's cooking and tossing the food on the floor. Vincent relived every slap, every drunken beating, every humiliation. He watched himself grow, under his father's tutelage, from a loving and trusting two-year-old into an 11-year-old bully who would deliberately maim a handicapped child and run away laughing, and then into a man who could not feel love and who believed that violence was the answer to every problem, especially with people he couldn't relate to.

It seemed to go on for hours, and Vincent knew his father was feeling and seeing every minute of it as he himself was reliving it.

When it was finally over, Vincent's father was bent over with his head in his hands, wailing. "Please, Vincent! Please forgive me."

Vincent would not have believed he could do it, but he reached out and put his hand on his father's back. When the old man straightened up, Vincent took him by the shoulders and looked directly into his eyes. "I forgive you. And you are forgiven. Both of those." Vincent wasn't sure where he got the authority to make that pronouncement, but he knew, as surely as he felt the weight of the universe lift from his shoulders, that it was true.

Vincent's father was crying from relief. "When your little brother gets here, you and I will both need to do some work with him. After that, we'll talk some more, okay? In there." He gestured toward the gates.

~~~~~~~

"Okay, Vincent, there's one more thing you need to see before you start your work, "said Eddy.

They moved away from Vincent's father and travelled in silence for a while.

"You know, Eddy, after I grew up I gave a lot of money to charities, groups that fed the hungry and helped the homeless and stuff."

"That's nice," replied Eddy.

"But doesn't it count?"

"What do you mean 'count'?"

"Well, sort of like time off for good behavior. You know, like maybe I get a little bit of a break for doing something good."

Eddy stopped. "Vincent, it doesn't work like that. This is not a balancing act, where an act of kindness toward one person cancels out an act of cruelty to another."

Eddy thought for a minute. "You know the self-help programs where they ask people to commit to a number of steps to help them overcome an addiction? There's one step where you 'make direct amends' to the people you've hurt if at all possible. They got that one exactly right. There's just no substitute for doing that.

"Anything you do to help someone else is pleasing to the Great Spirit, but it doesn't get you off the hook for having been a jerk at other times."

"Wait a minute," said Vincent. "I have a question."

"Good," said Eddy.

"God, Heavenly Father, Creator, Great Spirit -- which is it? What's His name?"

"All of them!" Eddy was laughing. "Yahweh, Great Spirit, Jehovah, Celestial Mother, Prime Mover, and many hundreds of others – I Am That I Am responds to all of them, along with several hundred names that have not been spoken on earth for tens of thousands of years. She even hears her name in the unarticulated feelings of longing and gratitude and awe experienced by young children and animals."

~~~~~~~

Eddy and Vincent were approaching a man who was holding the hands of a woman. Vincent recognized the undercut hair style and the Charlie-Chaplinesque toothbrush moustache immediately. Adolf Hitler was howling in terror, while the woman stoically watched him. He was crying out in German, but Vincent had no trouble understanding every word he said.

"That woman died in the gas chambers at Auschwitz," said Eddy, "along with her sister and her daughter. Adolf is experiencing exactly what she felt from the time she was herded, naked, into the chamber clasping her little daughter to her breast until the moment she died.

"The little boy in line behind her – the one in the green and white striped uniform with the yellow Star of David on the breast? – died of typhus at Bergen-Belsen. He was there at the same time as Anne Frank, by the way, and they were about the same age. The man behind him is a homosexual who was castrated, tortured, and finally starved to death at one of the other concentration camps."

Eddy paused. "There are never more than three people in Adolf's line, but as soon as he has completed his work with one of them, another one joins the line. Adolf has been doing this work 24 hours a day for almost 80 years now, and he's still working with the people who died before he did. After that, he will have to wait around to work with the people now living whose lives he shattered."

Vincent was stunned. Looking around, he recognized several other historical figures notorious for their cruelty. All of them were in agony, holding the hands of their victims. This seemed to be the lowest place in Purgatory.

Looking over his shoulder, Vincent could see the Pearly Gates in the distance. He wasn't sure whether being able to see the goal made things better or worse.

"How could you be here for any length of time without losing your mind?" he asked.

"It's not possible to lose your mind here," said Eddy. "Doing what they're doing is the only way out."

"Will Hitler get into Heaven?" asked Vincent.

"Eventually."

"Even he?"

"Even he."

Eddy and Vincent started back the way they had come.

~~~~~~~

"Here's your station, Vincent," said Eddy.

"I don't see anything," replied Vincent, looking around, "This spot looks exactly like everything else around here."

"Yes, but when you step into it, you will know that this is where you belong. At least for a while.

"This is where you will be working with the people you've hurt. From time to time, I will come and get you, and we'll go to someone who hurt you. It's usually someone who has just arrived, and you will help them see and feel what they did to you, very much like the work you did with your father.

Vincent looked toward the Pearly Gates and realized that there were a number of people coming toward him. Every one of them was coming to give him a chance to cleanse himself.

There was Mrs. Billings, whose flowers he had torn out of the ground in a rage after having been yelled at by his father. When she reported him to the police, Vincent had killed her cat, thrown the poor creature's body on her front porch, rung her doorbell, and waited around the corner of her house to hear her reaction. Even then, her cries had made him question his own actions, but he had never asked her forgiveness. Vincent knew that very soon he was going to feel all the grief he had caused her.

There was the girl he had raped in the back seat of his car. Oh, she had gotten in the back seat willingly enough, so that proved she really wanted it, right? Even after she said no and started crying, she was just being coy, right? At least that's what he told his friends when he was bragging to them about it the next day. She never told anyone, and Vincent never admitted what he knew in his heart, that he was guilty of an outrage. He couldn't even remember her name, but he knew that he was going to be reminded of it soon enough.

And there was his mother coming to him.

There were people approaching him from other places in Purgatory, people who were still doing their own work but were coming to help him with his. There was the geeky boy he had stuffed in his locker, the overweight girl Vincent had humiliated by pulling her skirt up in the school hallway and laughing at the size of her thighs, and many others.

Vincent also knew that, even when he had done his best to atone for what he had done to these people, there would be more. And more. And when he had done his work with all the people who had died before he did, he would be waiting here, in real earth time, for those who were still alive on earth.

Vincent closed his eyes and took a deep breath. He prayed for strength.

He opened his eyes and stepped into his place.

He had work to do.

SET FOR LIFE

After the national headlines and the local weather report predicting sunny skies and beautiful fall colors for this first week in October, the news anchor turned to the pretty young Special Features reporter. "I understand there's some exciting news about one very lucky Topekan, Bitsy."

"There sure is, Chad," Bitsy gushed. "There is a winner in the MegaMoolah lottery. As just about everyone knows, the prize had grown to 55 million dollars, and there is only one winning ticket this time. That means whoever is holding that ticket gets the whole thing! Well, after taxes, of course," Bitsy giggled. "The winning ticket was bought at the SpeedyShop on 21st Street, right here in Topeka, two days ago!"

"Do we know who the lucky winner is, Bitsy?" asked Chad.

"No one has come forward yet, Chad! But then, the winner has a year to claim the prize."

"Well, that *is* exciting news, Bitsy. Keep us informed, please."

"Whoever it is, they're set for life!" Bitsy flashed her perfect smile at the camera "Back to you, Chad."

~~~~~~

Abigail was one of those people who believe there's a right way to do everything. It wasn't that she always knew what the right way was, but she was convinced there was always a way to figure out what the right way was. There were few gray areas in Abigail's life.

Abigail just about forgot she had bought the lottery ticket. It had been an impulse purchase, bought when she had to go inside the SpeedyShop to get a receipt for her gasoline. If she weren't so obsessive about having a receipt for every purchase, if the gas station hadn't been out of receipt paper, if the clerk had been a little quicker, if the lottery ticket sign hadn't caught her eye, she wouldn't have become a multi-millionaire.

As it was, she didn't even think to check the ticket until she was watching the news two days later.

~~~~~~

The Thursday Pizza Lunch Bunch had been meeting every week for 4 years. It consisted of women who had known each other since high school and had kept in touch, off and on, ever since. Now they were all retired, and the group met regularly. They had seen each other through divorces, bankruptcies, menopause, re-marriages, job lay-offs, cancer scares, cancer realities, and the dwindling of the group from nine to five due to a move out of state, a big fight, and a death.

Abigail was the last to arrive that Thursday.

"My gosh, girl. We were just about to call you," said Linda. "And you look like crap. What's the matter with you?"

Abby sat down and rubbed her face with both hands. "I've been up all night," she whispered.

Danielle moved her chair back from the table. "Look, if you're sick, you go on home. I don't want to catch anything."

"I'm not sick, I just couldn't sleep," Abby assured them. "Something happened...I guess I should be excited and happy, but I'm just scared I'm going to mess this up...."

"Oh, my God, she met a man!" cried Crissy. "C'mon, tell, tell!"

The others leaned in, grinning.

"No, it's not that." Abby made the decision she had been struggling with for hours. "Okay, listen. This is really big, and you have to promise me you're not going to breathe a word of this to anyone. Anyone! Okay? I just don't want it to get out until I decide how to handle everything, how to do this right. But I have to tell someone before I come apart at the seams, okay? Promise!"

Four heads nodded agreement as they all leaned even closer.

Abby whispered, "I won the lottery."

There was silence while they waited for the punch line. When it was obvious Abby was serious, her four best friends leaned back in their chairs and stared at her.

"You mean like matching 5 numbers and winning a thousand dollars?" asked Gerry.

"No, the whole thing. Fifty-five million," said Abby, her voice beginning to shake.

Linda's eyes widened, she drew in a breath, and let out a whoop that turned every head in the room toward their table. Gerry and Danielle were squealing and laughing and bouncing in their chairs.

"Shut up!" whispered Abby, loudly enough for everyone at the nearby tables to hear. "I told you, I don't want this to get out!"

"Man, this is supposed to be happy time!" said Linda. "You should be jumping around and yelling! What's the matter with you?"

"You know," said Gerry, suddenly serious, "I've read about a lot of people who won big money, and just couldn't handle it. A year later they were broke and had to sell everything they bought just to pay the taxes. They just never end up very happy."

"That's not going to happen to our Abby," said Danielle. "She's smart and careful, and besides, she's going to share it all with her best friends so we'll all have the same problems, right?" She sent a big smile Abby's direction, and batted her eyelashes. "Right?"

Abby whimpered, "I don't know what to do. I've been up all night...."

"Okay, Abby! Here's what you do. You cash in that ticket, buy everything you've ever wanted, and have fun. It's that simple," said Linda.

"No, it's not that simple!" hissed Abby, suddenly angry. "According to the internet I'm supposed to hire a team of advisors – a tax accountant, a lawyer, a portfolio consultant, whatever that is. I have to decide whether to take the whole thing at once or some every year for the rest of my life. And I really, really don't want this getting out, because I don't want everyone in the world at my front door begging for handouts. But if I buy a big house and a new, fancy car and a bunch of expensive clothes and jewelry, how can I explain them? How long do you think it would take everyone to figure it out, huh?

"You don't understand." Abby was pleading. "I don't know how to explain it, but I just want to do this right. It's important that I do this right!"

There was a short silence before Gerry sighed, rubbed her eyes, and said, "You know, Abby, you have a really bad habit of thinking everything into the ground. You've just done what everyone in this country wants to do, and you're just bound and determined to turn it into a problem. I don't know what you mean by 'do it right,' but I'm going to be happy for you, even if you're not happy for yourself. So you just sit there with your head in your hands. I'm going to be happy enough for both of us."

"Well," said Abby after an embarrassed shrug, "I guess I could buy that nice birdbath I saw over at The Bird House."

Gerry, Danielle, Linda, and Abby laughed in relief. It wasn't until they heard the small sob that they realized Crissy hadn't said a word since the announcement. They all turned to her, confused. Danielle reached out to put her arm around Crissy's shoulder.

Crissy angrily shoved her arm away.

"Leave me alone!" she almost shouted. "This is so unfair! Jack and I have been buying tickets for years. Years! And the most we ever won was $500, and that doesn't even pay for all the tickets we bought." She glared at Abby with swollen eyes. "You _never_ buy lottery tickets. You _brag_ about how you never buy lottery tickets. 'Cause you're so smart and so good at math and you're just above it all and you know what the odds are and a bunch of crap like that. Then you go and buy one lousy ticket and win! This is just not fair!"

Abby decided she wouldn't offer to let them see the winning ticket after all.

~~~~~~

On her way home after lunch on Thursday, Abigail put the winning ticket in her safe deposit box.

On Friday morning Abigail called Crissy, but no one answered the phone. She left a message, but Crissy didn't call her back.

Friday afternoon, following advice she found on the internet, Abigail met with one of the officers at her bank to make sure there would be no question about transferring the money to her checking account. She called her attorney, the accountant who prepared her taxes every year, and her investment advisor. Telling them only that something big had happened, she set up a meeting for the four of them the following Monday afternoon at her attorney's office. She reminded all of them, several times, of their professional obligation to protect her privacy.

Over the weekend she did a lot of reading about the time-value of money, and studied everything she could find on whether to take the prize as a lump-sum or an annuity over the next 30 years.

She looked up the federal and Kansas state income tax rates for obscenely rich people.

It became clear very quickly that, at the age of 68, she would be a fool to do anything but take the lump-sum payment, even though it would cut her winnings almost in half. Invested properly, she would be able to more than make that up in a few years. And, with this particular lottery, if she were to die before the annuity was paid out, the money would stop; her heirs could not inherit whatever had not been paid. In 30 years she would be 98.

On Sunday morning she went to church, exhausted. Silently she gave thanks. Silently she asked for guidance. When it came time for praise announcements, she was silent. During fellowship after the service, several people asked if she was okay. She smiled a little and assured them she was fine, just a little tired.

On Sunday night she called her children. It was, she realized afterward, the first time in a week she had felt any real joy. Her sons cheered and laughed, her daughters-in-law cheered and laughed and cried, and all of them babbled on and on about the new cars and houses and geeky expensive toys they would be expecting for Christmas. Abby swore them to secrecy, then she hung up the phone and cried for half an hour. She cried out of joy, she cried out of love for her family, and she cried out of fear that she still might mess this up badly.

On Monday morning, she drove to the Bird House and bought a new bird bath.

On Monday afternoon she met with her "team of advisors," as it was called on the internet sites she had consulted – her attorney, her investment counselor, and her accountant. It was clear when she walked into the room that they had pretty well figured it out. After all, she had told them that "something big had happened," and every TV station in Topeka, as well as the newspaper, was breathlessly awaiting the identity of the big winner and taking every opportunity to keep the mystery in front of the public. As the receptionist ushered her into the conference room, she was met with three huge grins.

When she left the meeting two hours later, she had decided to take the lump sum of 28 million dollars. After federal, state, and local taxes, she would be left with about 18 million dollars.

She had made sure her will, at her death, would transfer her entire estate, after a few charitable bequests, to her sons and daughters-in-law.

She had made arrangements to provide for her grandchildren's college education.

She had made arrangements to provide a generous tax-free gift to each of her sons and each of her daughters-in-law every year during her lifetime.

She had made arrangements to establish a $5,000,000 charitable fund from which she could have anonymous contributions sent to whatever individuals or organizations she specified.

She had made arrangements to retain $1,000,000 in her checking account for a new car and a new house and new furniture and some new clothes and a whole great big bunch of new shoes.

She had made arrangements to establish a $5,000,000 fund which would automatically deposit $100,000 in her checking account every year.

She had made arrangements to invest the remaining 4 million.

For the first time since she realized she had won, she felt like she wasn't going to mess this up.

~~~~~~

On Tuesday morning Abigail walked nervously into the lottery offices and walked out a wealthy woman.

~~~~~~

On Wednesday Abigail looked at cars and contacted a real estate agent.

When she got home she sat down and paid off the entire balance on every one of her credit cards. When she was done, except for her mortgage, she didn't owe a cent to anyone. For quite a while she sat grinning at the spreadsheet where she kept careful track of every penny she owed, and which now showed zero balances for every creditor.

~~~~~~

On Thursday she went to Pizza Lunch Bunch as usual. She was the first one there, and for a while she was afraid no one else was coming. She sat there nervously fingering the four envelopes in her lap.

Linda was the next to arrive. She sat down grinning. "I assume you're buying today?"

"I guess I could do that," Abby smiled.

Gerry arrived and slipped into her usual chair. "Well, how's my very favorite rich bitch doing this week?" asked Gerry. "Are you over the shock yet? You look a lot better."

Crissy dragged in the door and sat down heavily. "So, have you decided to do the right thing?"

Abby looked quizzically at her. Crissy was obviously still angry.

"Well, how convenient of you to forget." The sarcasm was unmistakable. "But Danielle and I have been talking, and we both remember last year when we were sitting right here at this table and we all said that if any of us ever got rich we'd share with our friends."

Danielle had just come in, and had heard most of what Crissy had said. As she sat down she said, "Yeah, we did, Abby. We all sat here and promised. Didn't we?" She looked around the table. Crissy was nodding her head, and Gerry and Linda obviously had no idea what to say.

"Well, now that you mention it, I have made some arrangements for you," said Abby. She handed the envelopes around the table. "There's a check for each of you for $16,000 dollars. There's also a letter specifying that the money is a gift, so you don't have to pay any income tax on it. That's the most I can give you without you having to pay any tax."

Abby sat back, feeling pleased and generous. She watched as her best friends opened their envelopes and stared at the checks.

Finally Crissy looked up at her. "That's it? That's _it_? You're sitting on fifty-five million dollars, and we each get sixteen thousand? Seems to me you owe us at least ten million, lady! Fifty-five million split five ways is over ten million apiece." Danielle was nodding her head.

For a few seconds, Abby was speechless. She was aware that Linda and Gerry were looking at her, but she couldn't look away from Crissy's furious glare.

In the face of this outrage, ever-rational Abigail was trying to organize her thoughts.

Finally she laced her fingers together, hard, in front of her chest and leaned into the table. She spoke in a low, calm voice. "First of all, I'm not sitting on anywhere near fifty-five million. And even if I were, I made no such promise to any of you. No way on earth I'm giving any of you ten million dollars!"

"Look, Abby, Jack and I need that money!" Crissy pleaded.

"Jeesh, Crissy," said Gerry. "Abby doesn't have to give us anything. I kind of remember that day, too, but it was a joke! We were all just...."

"It was not a joke! It was a promise! If it were me, I'd keep my promise!" said Crissy, beginning to cry.

"Look, I don't know what kind of problems you're having, Crissy," began Abby, "but sixteen thousand dollars should help...."

"It's just a drop in the bucket," said, Crissy, crying hard now. "You owe me ten million dollars!"

"Do you have any idea the amount of good I could do with ten million dollars?" wailed Danielle.

"And I can't?" growled Abby through clenched teeth. "You don't think I know how to do some good, too? In fact, I thought these checks were the beginning of my doing a _lot_ of good, but I guess I was wrong."

Abby got up and walked quietly out of the restaurant.

Nobody had even ordered pizza.

~~~~~~

Abigail was never sure how the secret got out, but get out it did. The officers at her bank were probably trustworthy, but the young bank teller who processed the payment when it came in may have been unable to keep from telling her boyfriend that night. It was even possible that the receptionist in her lawyer's office mentioned it to his wife. But Abby always suspected that Crissy, still in tears from what she thought of as the unfairness of the situation, had told Jack the minute she got home from that first lunch.

Topeka is too big for everyone to know everyone else, but at 126,000 people, the degrees of separation are few. Name all your acquaintances in front of any group of people, and every person in the group is sure to know 3 or 4 of them. Crissy's husband Jack, for example, regularly played golf with one of the men in Abby's church.

However it happened, when Abby walked into church that next Sunday she noticed people talking in groups and glancing at her over their shoulders, and she knew the secret was out. A couple of people walked up and said, exaggeratedly and loudly, "So, Abby, how you doing?" while everyone around them laughed. Pastor Ken, standing in the aisle and socializing before the service, said, "Hey, did you hear the big lottery winner claimed the prize and chose to remain anonymous? I wonder why anyone would want to do that!" And everyone laughed. The chair of the Stewardship Committee walked by, coughed into her hand, a cough that sounded a lot like, "tithe." And everyone laughed.

At fellowship after the service, Abigail was headed for the refreshment table when she heard her name being called, too loudly, from across the room. "Abby, come over here a minute! There's someone I want you to meet!" called Mary, a woman Abby barely knew. As Abby walked over, Mary was tugging a visibly uncomfortable man in her direction.

"Abby, I'd like you to meet my brother, Jim."

Jim was maybe 50, painfully shy, unsure what to do with his eyes and hands.

"Hi, Jim." Abby offered her hand. "I don't think I've seen you here before. Is this your first visit to our church?"

Jim's reply was all but inaudible.

"Here, Abby, sit down with us, why don't you. Jim, help Abby with her chair, okay?" suggested his sister.

Jim wasn't quite sure how to do that, but he did his best.

"Jim, why don't you go get Abby and yourself some refreshments?"

As soon as he was away from their table, Mary leaned over and whispered to Abby, "I know Jim doesn't present himself well, but

SHARON ANN HARPER DUBOIS

he really wanted to meet you. He was telling me how much he enjoyed the anthem the choir sang, and how beautiful your voice is. I think he's quite taken with you!" Mary winked at Abby.

"He could hear me singing? I mean me, individually?" asked Abby. "The choir director should have signaled me to quiet down some. And is Jim usually taken with average-looking, overweight women 15 or 20 years older than he is?"

Mary reddened and stammered, "Well, I must say you don't look that old, and, well, Jim is older than he looks, really...."

Abby was staring at her.

"You know," said Mary, "I was just trying to do something nice for you. I know how lonely you must be since your divorce, and Jim is such a nice man."

Jim was back, and plopped a plate piled with five brownies, a bunch of grapes, a large handful of mints, and a donut in front of Abby. He dropped gracelessly into a chair and started eating from his own plate. He didn't look at Abby or speak to her.

"Where in the world did you get the idea I'm lonely?" Abby asked Mary, trying to smile. "I assure you, in the fifteen years I've been divorced, I have never been lonely. And in all the years we've been going to this church together, this is the first time you've shown any concern about my social life. I can't imagine what has changed, what brought this all on. Can you tell me?"

Abby waited through 7 or 8 seconds of dreadful silence before turning to Jim. "Jim, it was nice to meet you. I hope you'll come back and visit again." Abby stood, picked up her plate laden with an entire day's worth of calories and moved to another table.

~~~~~~

On Tuesday Abby's financial advisor called and told her the checks for her charitable fund had arrived. Abby drove to the advisor's office and made out the paperwork for generous, anonymous donations to be made to the Everywoman's Resource Center, Washburn University, the Rescue Mission, her church, the Community Resources Council, Let's Help, Doorstep, and Cornerstone.

~~~~~~

For years Abby had had a picture of her dream house floating around in her head. Since she had always assumed she would never actually own such a house the picture was fuzzy at best.

When she had contacted the realtor who helped her find her current townhome, she had explained to him pretty much what she was looking for. She assumed, though, that she'd end up having to build something to get what she wanted, but she was wrong. Carl called her on Wednesday and asked if she was available on Thursday to visit a place he thought she'd like.

It was perfect. It was brand new and custom built, finished but not yet decorated. The previous owners had built their dream home, then got transferred back east somewhere before they could even move in. It was sleek and modern. There were four bedrooms, five bathrooms, a sunroom, a dining room big enough to seat twelve, a pantry the size of a small bedroom, state-of-the-art appliances, a deck overlooking a yard where Abby would plant lovely flower gardens. There was a perfect place for her new birdbath. There was plenty of room for lots of shoes.

It was a lot bigger than she needed, of course, but there would be plenty of room when her family came to visit. She could throw parties without worrying where everyone would sit. She pictured herself hosting events that everyone in Topeka would want to attend.

The same house, on either coast, would have cost more than she had budgeted. But in Topeka, even with a basement for tornado protection and excellent insulation against Midwestern winters, housing is comparatively affordable.

SHARON ANN HARPER DUBOIS

She told Carl to start on the paperwork. She told him she would pay cash.

When she got home she called and made an appointment with the decorator whose work she had always admired – the one she had thought she could never afford.

It wasn't until she hung up that she realized it was Pizza Thursday, and she had forgotten to go.

~~~~~~

On Saturday Abby signed her name to a stack of papers and a large check, and Carl handed her the keys to her new house. It's amazing how quickly things can move when there's a lot of cash changing hands.

~~~~~~

Abigail couldn't remember exactly when Francis had started coming to church. He didn't seem to know anyone there, always sat at the outside end of the pew, alone. If someone sat down close to him and tried to engage him in conversation before the service, he got up and moved. During the service he stood when everyone else stood and sat when everyone else sat, but that was the extent of his participation. He didn't sing the hymns, didn't even open a hymnal. During fellowship he ate a lot, and often went through the line more than once, but he took his plate to a far corner of the room and didn't respond to friendly overtures. His clothes were ragged and none too clean.

On Sunday, Abby waited until Francis was about to leave the building, hurried over to him, handed him an envelope, and quickly walked away.

In the envelope was $500 in 20-dollar bills.

~~~~~~

Over the next several days, Abby began to get used to the feeling of being rich. She no longer woke up several times each night, either smiling at the feeling of more money than she could spend, or in a panic from half-remembered dreams of catastrophic loss.

She took possession of her new Lexus LX. She paid cash for it.

She met with her decorator and spent two hours oohing and aahing her way through catalogs of luscious sofas, stunning light fixtures, and eye-popping dinnerware. Abby couldn't even wait until the new house was completely furnished to move in. The new bedroom furniture she had chosen was available for delivery on Saturday, and she decided to move as soon as it was in place.

After all, she didn't have to wait until her current house sold. She could afford to own two houses at once.

Gerry and Linda called, and the three of them met for lunch. Her friends told Abby how much they appreciated her generosity and told her excitedly some of the things they planned to do with her gifts to them. They admired her new car, and she told them about the new house. They never mentioned money again. Instead, they talked about Gerry's new granddaughter and smiled over the pictures. They decided the baby looked a lot like Gerry except around her eyes, which she obviously got from the other side of the family. Linda told them she was exhibiting two paintings at a North Topeka Arts District gallery. The three of them arranged to go up there the following week for lunch and a walk around the various shops and galleries.

Abby's life began to feel normal again. Just richer.

~~~~~~

On Friday she drove to Kansas City to have dinner with her children and grandchildren. Abby had long known that her relationship with her sons and their wives and children was one of the great blessings of her life. Not only did she get along well with all of them, but they seemed to all like and respect each other.

She figured, if she had done nothing else right in her life, her contribution to their current well-being was a triumph.

She had asked them to make reservations at their favorite expensive restaurant. They beamed and rushed to hug her when she walked in. The twins wanted to know if they were all millionaires now. Abby replied, "I am. You're not." All eight of them laughed, but Abby thought her sons exchanged questioning glances with their wives.

After they were seated and had ordered, Abby got down to business. She had a stack of official-looking envelopes, and she handed one each to five-year-old Robert and Michael and sixteen-year-old Antonia.

"First of all," Abby began, "I'm handing these to you because they actually belong to you; However, I strongly suggest that as soon as you've had a look at them you turn them over to your parents for safekeeping.

"I've established a college trust fund for each of you in the amount of half a million dollars each. In those envelopes is all the paperwork you need to claim the money when the time comes. The money will be administered by the fund. You can use it for tuition, supplies, fees, and all reasonable living expenses, and it will be doled out to you as needed.

"Now, here's the important part. When you graduate, when you earn a four-year degree, whatever remains in the trust fund becomes yours. You can use it to start a business, or to live on while you look for a job, or – what I hope you'll do – you can use it to go to graduate school.

"You'll never get a need-based scholarship now, but if you can get one based on merit, or if you choose to work part time while you're in school, there will be just that much more money left for you. It will be your choice.

"Now, here's the catch. If you don't graduate, or if you don't go to college at all, you get only half of the fund, and you don't get it until you're forty."

"Forty!" said Michael.

"Yep," said Abby. If you don't go to college you'll have to make a living for yourself until you're that old. If that's the path you choose, believe me, you'll appreciate the money when it finally comes to you."

The waiter brought their food.

Newly-licensed-to-drive Antonia asked, "Can I have a car instead?"

"Not a chance," said Abby, grinning. Then she realized Antonia was serious.

Antonia turned to her mother. "You said I could have a car!"

Clearly flustered, Kim told Antonia to quiet down, that they would talk about it later.

Antonia pouted the rest of the evening.

Abby handed each of the adults an envelope.

"You know," she said, "I could hand each of you a big wad of cash, and I really thought about it. If you were struggling financially I probably would. But all of you have good jobs, and I've relieved you of the need to save for your kids' college education. That should be a big help to you. She glanced meaningfully at Antonia.

"What I've done is establish another fund that will pay each of you $16,000 per year for the rest of my life. That's the most I can give you without creating a taxable event, as my accountant calls it. That's $32,000 extra income, tax free, per family. When I'm gone you will all inherit, after a few charitable bequests, my estate. Then you can retire in luxury. But not yet. Not in your thirties and early forties."

"I don't know why not," muttered Stewart.

"Well," said Raymond, "we know you didn't have to give us anything. So we're grateful for all of this." It was said with a great deal less enthusiasm than Abby had anticipated.

"Hold on a minute, Mom," said Stewart. "You're giving the same amount to each of your grandchildren? Antonia starts college in a year, but it will be twelve or thirteen years before Raymond's twins graduate high school. Their funds will have time to grow, so, really, you've given them a lot more than you've given Antonia."

"Oh, what difference does it make," snapped Raymond. "They can all go to college. And college will probably be more expensive in twelve years than it is now."

"I'm just saying," said Stewart.

Kim and Helen told their husbands to back off.

"I thought we were all going to be millionaires," said Robert.

"Okay, then," said Abby, with less joy than she had thought she would feel, "my next suggestion is that we all go on a vacation together next summer. All eight of us. My treat. What do you think? Where shall it be?"

The group perked up a bit as they discussed the relative merits of Yellowstone, the Grand Canyon, an inland waterway cruise to Alaska, and Disneyland.

~~~~~~

On Saturday she trailed the delivery men into her new bedroom as they carried in her gorgeous new bed, dresser, night stands, lamps and mattress. She made up the bed with her luxurious new sheets and comforter, and considered herself at home.

~~~~~~

When the choir stood to sing the anthem on Sunday, Abby glanced over the congregation. She noticed that, far from sitting alone,

Francis was surrounded by ten or twelve people. They were all looking directly at her and whispering among themselves. They were loud enough that a number of those sitting near them glanced over disapprovingly.

After the service, while she was hanging up her choir robe and putting on her suit coat, Abby considered skipping fellowship and going straight home, but she enjoyed the company and the conversation of the fellowship hour so much she decided to head downstairs.

She never even made it to the refreshment table. As soon as she stepped off the bottom stair she was surrounded. Most of the group looked as if they had come straight from the Rescue Mission. They might even have spent the night under the Kansas Avenue Bridge. No one greeted her or introduced herself, no one offered his hand. They were all talking at once and crowding around her.

"...mother is really sick...", "...haven't eaten since Friday....", "...really need some help....", "...Francis said....", "...pay the rent....", "...gonna lose my car...."

Abby had a moment of panic when she knew what an antelope surrounded by hungry lions must feel like. She had backed up until she could feel the wall behind her. She started to explain to them about the charitable foundation she had established, but they couldn't hear her and they wouldn't have cared. All they knew was that Francis had gotten a lot of cash from her and there was no reason she couldn't do the same for every one of them. Abby couldn't make herself heard above them, and she had no place to go. She resorted to shouting at them.

"STOP IT!" she yelled. "I can't help you! Don't you understand? I can't help you! I can't help everybody! I can't give everybody exactly what they want exactly when they want it! I'm trying to do this right, but nothing I do is enough! There isn't enough money in the world to give everyone everything they want!"

There was silence in the room as several of the congregation elbowed their way through the crowd, took Abby by the arms and escorted her to a table. Shaken and near tears, she sat long enough to catch her breath. Then she fled.

~~~~~~

Abby fled to Gage Park.

She parked by the rose garden and sat in her car and cried for a while. Since there hadn't been a hard freeze yet, the roses were still beautiful. Armed with a handful of tissues, Abby walked around the garden sniffling. She made her way to the rock garden, sat on a bench, and cried some more.

She began to feel a little better. The air was crisp and the leaves were beautiful and Abby kept walking. As she passed the carousel she smiled at the music and the children waiting in line. She took the path around the Victorian Garden, then sat at a picnic table for a while. As the sun inched downward it became clear that it was going to be chilly. She thought about those people at church. Would the Rescue Mission have enough beds tonight? How cold would it be under the bridge tonight? She didn't know. She had made a generous contribution to the Mission. Would it help very much? She didn't know. How could those people be made aware of her charitable fund? She didn't know.

She really, truly didn't know what to do.

Sitting at the picnic table she cried some more. Then, with her head in her hands, she dozed off. When she lifted her face the sun was noticeably lower. She stood up wearily and began to make her way back to her car.

As she passed the carousel, a sudden gust of wind sent a shower of golden leaves swirling around her. It looked for all the world as if she were being showered with gold coins. She closed her eyes, stretched her arms out, and began to turn slowly around and around. When she stopped and opened her eyes a group of preschoolers and their parents were smiling at her.

She smiled back. "Look! It's raining money on me! I'm rich! I'm rich!"

The children rushed forward and began to dance in the falling leaves. "I'm rich! I'm rich!" they called out as they twirled and danced.

Suddenly Abby was more tired than she could remember ever being in her life.

Abigail drove her beautiful, new, expensive car to her beautiful, new, expensive house and locked it in the garage. She went inside, locked all the doors, and set the alarm. She drew the blinds. She locked the greedy world out, and she locked her selfish self in, and she went to bed.

PESTILENCE

A nd so, feeling the need for companionship, God created the angels. God loved the angels, and the angels loved God.

"Almighty Creator, shall we soar around you with our eyes and feet covered? Shall we call to one another, 'Holy, holy, holy?'"asked one of the angels.

"Why would I want that?" smiled God. "I am omniscient, so I know what I am. I am also omnibenevolent, so I want for you something more fulfilling than that. Let's make something interesting instead."

So God reached out, and from a speck of nothingness sprang the entire physical universe. And God touched the minds of the angels, and they were able to see that what had been only energy was cooling into matter. They could understand that there were laws that governed both the energy and the matter. And the angels understood why the laws were necessary.

"Loving Creator, if things don't go the way you want, will you change the laws of this universe?" asked one of the angels.

"No, I won't," answered God. "You will come to understand that these laws are more complex than you can see right now. The laws are necessary and sufficient for any eventuality."

The angels watched in awe as matter formed itself into particles, and the particles swirled and rotated around each other and clumped together into groups of two or three or dozens, and arranged themselves in beautiful patterns.

"Why do they do that?" asked the angels. So God touched the minds of the angels, and they could see and understand positive and negative charges. God taught the angels about the laws that created particles and atoms and molecules. And the angels understood why they were necessary. And God and the angels loved everything about the particles.

The angels could see that space was curved around large accumulations of matter so that smaller pieces fell toward them. Sometimes they collided, and sometimes the smaller ones began to circle around the larger.

"Loving Parent, why are the large accumulations of matter almost perfectly round?" the angels asked. So God touched the minds of the angels, and they understood that, of all the solids, a sphere has the smallest surface area for its volume. And they could see how the laws of the universe had made it so. And the angels understood why it was necessary.

So God and the angels admired the exploding stars, spewing complex chemicals into the space around. They watched as the exploded stars sometimes shrank into points so dense that light could not escape, and whose massive gravity pulled stars and planets into beautiful, swirling galaxies around them. And God and the angels loved the stars and the planets and the galaxies and the black holes.

"Dear God," said one of the angels, "I see that most of the planets are so near their stars that all the gasses around them have burned away, including water. Or else they are so far away and so cold that all their water is solid."

"Yes. Aren't they beautiful?" said God. "Look how perfect and pristine they are. They are not unchanging, though. They have volcanoes and lava flows and geysers, and even collisions with comets and asteroids. They dance and sing and reform themselves constantly." And God and the angels loved the pristine planets.

"Oh, God!" said one of the angels. "On one of the cold planets, in the liquid under the ice, some of the very large molecules have started to reproduce! They are making copies of themselves from other particles in the liquid!"

"And now we have life," said God. "When complex molecules are able to replicate themselves from material around them, we call it life."

"Do you love the life, Dear God?" asked an angel.

"I love all my creation," replied God. So the angels loved the life, too.

The angels watched, fascinated, as the life molecules accumulated the material they needed, lined up the atoms just so, then released the newly-formed copies of themselves.

"Creator God," said one of the angels, "some of the life molecules are disintegrating. Why does that happen?"

"That's another of the laws of the universe I have created. Any life that reproduces must die. If they replicated themselves and lived forever, soon there would not be enough material to sustain them. And since they have no control over their urge to reproduce, after a time they must die." And the angels understood why that was necessary. And the angels also understood that because God allowed life to die did not mean God loved life any less.

"Oh, God! Oh, God! Oh, God!" cried an angel, horrified. "Over there, on that warmer planet, life has begun. But the life molecules aren't reproducing from free-floating particles. They're tearing the other life molecules apart so they can use the parts to make copies of themselves!" And the angels watched in horror as the life molecules fought and grappled and ripped and killed each other.

In time, groups of molecules found ways to team up and specialize so that some of them grabbed their prey and some of them ripped the prey apart, and some of them distributed the dismembered prey to the entire group. The life molecules organized themselves into cells and organs and organisms. They found ingenious ways to reproduce themselves within the safety of their bodies before sending their offspring out to perpetuate the cycle.

And God showed the angles that, for life, killing was necessary for survival.

Some of the organisms came out of the water to live on land and breathe air, and some stayed in the water. In all their forms, they reproduced so successfully that they populated the entire planet, and they continued to rip and tear and kill each other in order to ensure their own survival.

"Creator God," said one of the angels, "I see that as the new-formed stars spin and throw off matter that will become planets, they make the same pattern as the whirling galaxies. It's the same pattern some of the organisms have developed for their protective shells and some for their growing seeds." So God caused the angels to see the sacred geometry, the golden mean, and its resulting spiral. And the angels understood why it was necessary.

Finally the angels come to God, grief-stricken.

"Dear God," they cried, "we know you are a benevolent creator and that you love all your creation. But life has grown so large, so sophisticated, that its technology is going to allow it to leave its home planet. It's planning to spread its greed, its violence, its rapaciousness, its pollution, to other planets. It's planning to reform the beautiful, pristine planets near its own so it can live on them. We also know you said you would never break the laws of the universe you created, that the laws you made when you brought everything into existence from nothingness are necessary and sufficient for any situation. But we beg you, please step in and stop this pestilence from spreading beyond the planet where it was born!"

"My beloved angels," smiled God, "do you not yet understand? Look at the technology life has developed. Do you not see that every bit of technology that can be used to move life from one planet to another can also be used for destruction? Life was born a killer, and a killer it must remain to survive. The organisms have been fighting among themselves – constantly – since their ancestors lined up atoms into molecules. It's one of the laws of my universe.

"It's another law of my universe that the technology life believed it would use to leave its home planet, it will use instead to destroy itself."

And the angels understood why that was necessary.

CONVERSATION
WITH MY BLADDER

"Get up and pee! Get up and pee!"
My too-full bladder calls to me.

All snug and warm in bed, I say,
"Nope. This is where I'm going to stay."

"You know you cannot put this off.

What if you have to sneeze? Or cough?
You can't go back to sleep instead,
And if you try, you'll wet the bed."

I moan and whine, "I just don't wanna!"
She answers back, "You know you're gonna!"

"It's cold out there!" I loudly grouse.

"Outside it's cold, but in your house
You know your furnace works just fine.
The temperature is sixty-nine."

"It's way too far!" The mood is tense.
That argument makes little sense.

"Your forebears used a chamber pot,
And you complain because you've got
To walk twelve feet to get relief.
So tell me, is it your belief
It's better, as they did, in skivvies
To trudge across the fields to privies?"

The urge to pee grows ever stronger.
I can't procrastinate much longer.
I toss the blankets and the sheet,
And on the carpet plant my feet.
I can't continue with the chatter.
I make the trek, I void my bladder,
Return to bed, and slumber beckons.
I'm back to sleep in seven seconds.

The inconvenience is slight
And yet I argue every night.

She does her job. She knows what's best
For me, and 'though I need my rest
I know I'm madder than a hatter
To argue with my faithful bladder.

How much more calm my life would be
If with my bladder I'd agree
That when she first calls out to me
I'd simply get me up, and pee.

ACKNOWLEDGEMENT AND AUTHOR'S NOTES

The concept of choosing your own government and the title Tier Zero are the brainchild of my son Steven. When he finally tired of my pestering him to write the book and told me (kindly, of course) to do it myself, I jumped at the chance. The finished product on these pages is an entirely different story from the one he would have written, but the original concept was all his.

The Topeka depicted in Tier Zero and Set for Life is the Topeka of 2023. The timeline of Tier Zero stretches 50-plus years into the future, and I am well aware that the named streets, neighborhoods, landmarks, industrial areas and shopping districts will certainly have changed by then. But we are advised to write what we know, and the Topeka I know is the Topeka of 2023. Those of you who are still around in 2079 are welcome to write a preface detailing those changes for whatever edition of this book comes out that year.

Some of the material in this book has already appeared on the author's blog "The Joyful Cynic."

ABOUT THE AUTHOR

Sharon Ann Harper Dubois

Sharon is the child of an Air Force family. She has lived in Texas, Oklahoma, California, England, and Germany. She currently lives in Topeka, Kansas. She holds a BA in mathematics from Washburn University.

Sharon served for several years as vice chair of the Libertarian Party of Kansas. She is currently co-chair of Libertarians of Northeast Kansas.

Sharon is a fan of Gilbert and Sullivan, and helped found the Gilbert and Sullivan Society of Kansas, better known as GaSS-Kan.